SEEKER'S CALL

Book One of the Seeker's Trilogy

CASSANDRA BOYSON

www.CassandraBoyson.com

DEDICATED TO
Victoria and Steven

CONTENTS

❧ I ❧

FOLLOWING A WORN, rock-encrusted road, Iviana set her course for the capital city of the young, tenacious Kierelian kingdom found upon the planet Kaern. She had always lived within the borders of this land, but had ventured into little of it in all the years of her quiet life.

Iviana had neither reason nor desire to visit the heart of the kingdom, but chose her destination because she had nowhere else to go. Desperation had driven her to leave the cottage of her former mentor and friend, Naphtali. Even so, now she was free of the pressing walls of that house, she had no more direction than before her departure.

It was on this well-worn road that a scene familiar to Iviana's dreams appeared. Gazing to her left, she recognized the huge cedar with gnarly, exposed roots, though she had never visited the place

1

before. It appeared as though it were being used as a sort of living, standing nurse log, covered with a plethora of winding foliage that used it to climb higher in its longing to reach the rays of the life-giving sun.

As Iviana ambled up to the aged tree, a pure white dove flew down and perched itself on one of the lower branches, eye level with Iviana. The dove, too, had haunted Iviana's dreams. It was this very picture she recalled entering her sleep over past years. In fact, the young woman could not remember when the dream had begun—only that she had always known it—and now the vision was set before her, in her waking life, she was not necessarily surprised.

Peering into the face of the dove, Iviana felt as though her feet were held fast to the ground. It did not possess the countenance of a mere bird, but was much more. The young woman felt the urge to kneel before it in its obvious majesty, but suppressed it.

The dove turned head over shoulder, then gazed back at her for a moment before flying in the direction it had gestured. Iviana felt it wished her to follow and she, quite irrationally, wished to do so, but couldn't help feeling this was foolhardy. She tried to force her feet into walking back toward the road, but they betrayed her and carried her in the direction the dove had exited, though not before she noticed the glittering golden dust it had left behind on the tree branch. Bemused as well as intrigued, her legs moved swiftly.

After traveling for miles with no more than odd traces of its gleaming gold-dust as a trail, Iviana stopped to catch her breath and realized she must give up her search of the majestic feathered creature. It had ultimately disappeared and obviously wasn't keen on returning to her.

Beholding the surrounding landscape, it was anything but inviting. What could be seen beyond the sleepy mist that had gathered around her when the sun had begun to set was a dry, barren wilderness, orange the shade of decaying pumpkin and covered with naught but boulders and vegetation she knew grew only in desolate regions.

She then looked to the dimming sky. The sun would soon be hidden, but she was too weary to make the return journey to the road. *I suppose this is as good a place as any to stop for the night*, she thought, irritated she had come this far for nothing—feeling foolish she had allowed herself the inane chase.

Squinting through the fog, she could make out a clear space of land between two large boulders that would be comfortable for an evening's rest. Whistling merrily at her good fortune, she was making her way around one of the large rocks when she noticed some movement. She quickly tucked herself behind the dusty rock and eased her head around it to peek at whatever lay beyond.

Gasping at what she beheld, Iviana blinked a few times to check her vision. What lay in the dry, flat clearing was a creature she had always dreamed of encountering, but had never actually thought the dream could possibly come true.

It was a dragon, or what Iviana believed was a dragon as she had never seen one outside the pages of a book. It was a large, fierce creature, but also graceful and surprisingly beautiful. It reminded her of a fluid deer or lithe horse rather than a snake or other creatures she had heard dragons compared to.

The beast stood, perched on hind legs, with large, billowing wings folded back. Its long neck stretched toward the sky and its eyes were gleaming in the retreating sunlight. Those eyes were mesmerizing. Iviana had only ever heard dragon eyes described as full of flame or black and iniquitous. These descriptions were either largely exaggerated however, or this was not a dragon, for the set of eyes before her were almost human, aside from the lack of whites that human eyes possess. They were a set of large, black pupils surrounded by a ring of incredibly piercing green.

With a body cloaked in pale greens and blues with white spotting scattered over its back and feet, it produced the effect of a spring day, though there was no escaping the intimidation that emanated from the creature. This aspect was not so spring-like.

Seeing the dragon before her filled Iviana with such wonder she forgot her every trouble: her recent sorrow, her lonely, aimless wandering and the fruitless quest for the dove. Feelings akin to the spirited sounds of a flute she had once heard resounded exuberantly inside her. Here, at the end of her foolish path, in this desolate place, was a creature few could claim to have seen in her lifetime, though sightings had been more numerous in earlier decades.

The first she had ever heard of a dragon was when her mentor, Naphtali, had taken time to show her one in a book. Yet uncertain of Naphtali's purpose, Iviana had found it beautiful and, at her reaction, Naphtali had seemed pleased and continued to explain what she knew of the creatures, how grand and regal they were when one was before you.

Iviana had inquired when her shut-in companion had ever been near a dragon, but Naphtali changed the subject and it had never been broached again. After this introduction, even when Iviana heard tales of their destructive tendencies, she was filled with interest at the thought of such a powerful animal.

Nonetheless, Iviana was naturally frightened of the one that stood tall before her. That did not mean she was going to flee, however. She began to draw herself nearer to it, almost in a trance, mesmerized by intrigue. There was an unidentifiable pull between the dragon and herself that, in the very back of her mind, she wondered the dragon did not feel as well and turn her way. Still, it was in her best interest that it did not, for she would probably flee.

Iviana, entranced, continued forward, wanting to touch its smooth, sleek skin or communicate with it somehow—to connect with this magnificent being—but a noise that both snapped Iviana out of her stupor and captured the creature's attention resonated from beyond the boulders on the opposite side of the clearing. Suddenly appearing ten times fiercer, the dragon's body became completely rigid and the emerald rings around its pupils grew dark.

The pair waited breathlessly for something to emerge, but after some time, without even the smallest sound following the first occurrence, the dragon dismissed it and its eyes grew brighter again. After releasing a long, fatigued breath, it curled up on the ground with front and hind legs tucked close like a cat.

Iviana was not so easily convinced they were alone. She knew what she had heard: a gasp and a shuffling of feet as though someone had lost their footing and, whoever it was, they had seen this incredible creature as well. She began to creep back behind the large rocks that she might make her way to where the other was without alerting the dragon to her presence.

It was a tougher trek than she had been expecting. There was not much cover and the ground was full of gravel, making it hard to keep silent. Twice, she nearly slid across the dry, clay-ridden ground and the only rocky cover she was able to find was nearer the dragon than she cared to be.

Eventually, a movement in the boulders caught her attention. She spotted a young man, perhaps her own age or a little older, all in brown as though he had dressed to camouflage himself within a forest. It did not do him much good in this area, though, surrounded entirely by red-orange ground and rock, so she assumed he had not meant to come so far out of the woods. He had a full head of brown hair crowning a face with strikingly intense eyes and was climbing over and around rock after rock with obvious expertise.

She wondered if this man was one of the great dragon-hunters she had heard about. Several of the king's knights had been knighted for slaying dragons. But if the man was a hunter, could she let him slay this dragon? She would make use of the sword she carried, if need be, but did she want the dragon to live? She'd heard tell of them rampaging whole towns and villages and even the kingdom's first royal fortress had been destroyed by them. Nevertheless, how could she be certain those stories were true? After all, this dragon was nothing like all she had heard described. She had read several books on what knights and dragon-hunters had shared about them, along with narratives of those who had come across dragons by surprise, though these cases were rare. Over the past hundred years or so, dragons had become quite scarce and only those who wished to make themselves heroes sought them out.

Iviana risked a glance over her boulder. The dragon had curled its head comfortably against its body, completely unaware of the humans stalking it. When she looked back to the man, he was completely vulnerable, no longer needing to hide, for the dragon seemed to be falling asleep. Still, he moved slowly and silently, closer and closer to the creature.

What is he doing? Iviana wondered. She contemplated whether he was as taken with the dragon as she and only desired a better glimpse of its magnificence.

She made ready to stand and show the young man that she, too, was there, when he pulled the sword from the scabbard at his side and leaped at the beast.

Iviana stood, desperately screaming, *"No!"* This dragon would not be slain, if she could help it.

The dragon raised its head and turned in the direction from where it had heard Iviana's exclamation. It showed evidence it was ready to defend itself with hundreds of sharp teeth gleaming at the two humans who had crept up on it, but before Iviana could finish her cry, the man lunged with the sword and struck the flesh in the dragon's side.

The stranger dared a glance in her direction after his strike. The look he gave her was of astonishment, a trace of anger, but mostly curiosity. Iviana thought she recognized a shred of sorrow as well. Nevertheless, he shrugged her off and focused on the dragon as it attempted to bring itself to a full stand, but the animal stumbled to the ground, smoke floating from its nostrils. It did not release flame, as Iviana had so often heard described.

The young man attempted to strike again when Iviana finally snapped from her stupor and raced to the dragon's defense. She leaped before the raised sword, shielding the dragon, and lifted her own blade to block the astounded man's blow. Her attempt was successful, but she was ready at any moment for the dragon to rid itself of her presence. She had wanted to be near the dragon, but not so close her back was held firmly against the creature's side.

The young man looked down at her with sparkling, stunned eyes. "What are you doing?" he asked.

"Stopping you," she spat back the obvious.

"It's already injured," he retorted. "The least you could do is let me finish it off." He moved his sword to take a blow at its head, but she deflected his attempt.

"No!" she yelled, fervency filling her voice. "*Look* at it! What has this dragon done to you?"

He stepped back and stumbled over a rock, nearly falling on his back. "I need it. I need its heart," he managed to mutter with an expression that looked rather kindred to remorse.

Why would a dragon-hunter feel regret? she wondered. Still, Iviana looked him over a moment. She didn't know why he *needed* this beautiful creature's heart, but it was of no consequence.

A sudden attack with her sword caught him off guard and she had an easy time pushing him away from the dragon, but it soon became apparent he was talented with his weapon and she was not certain she would survive the attack she had placed on him.

"Why are you defending it?" he asked angrily, though genuinely curious.

She ignored his question and pressed harder, but the man was desperate and eventually flung the sword from Iviana's hands, casting her body to the ground. She lay back to the ground with hands out in surrender, ready for him to strike. With eyes closed, she waited for the inevitable, but when nothing happened, she opened them again.

He was running back to where the dragon lay.

Desperately, she raced to the dragon as well. The young man raised his sword over the dragon's neck. Lacking time to formulate a wiser plan, Iviana flung herself over the dragon's large neck and cried, *"Please!"*

The attacker halted just before his weapon

would have been cast upon her flesh.

Iviana looked into his dark eyes and watched a series of thoughts and emotions riddle his face before he threw his sword to the ground.

She blinked, surprised.

"It's going to die anyway," he said in a low voice. "I hear they don't heal well."

Iviana thought a moment. "I'm going to heal it," she replied with sudden determination.

He gave a short, cheerless laugh and asked, "And how are you going to do that?"

She turned to examine the dragon's wound. It was deep, but the animal was breathing fine, if a little shakily from the pain it was experiencing. She didn't believe anything vital had been struck, though she knew nothing of dragon anatomy.

"Why do you care?" she asked, turning back to where the stranger had been, but he and his sword had vanished. "Good riddance!" she shouted to the horizon.

ജ 2 ൽ

TVIANA TURNED TO the dragon and looked wearily into its face. It, too, was looking at her, or inside of her and reading her, so she felt. Its nose continued bleeding smoke, but its eyes were greener than ever, as though pain had inflamed them. The dragon laid its head upon the ground.

With time to think, the reality of her situation was becoming clear. She knew nothing about dragons or their healing process. No one had ever attempted to heal a dragon before—at least not to her knowledge. She did, however, have experience in doctoring a number of other animals such as horses, rabbits, dogs and cats. Even a few wounded birds had received care from her and her mentor, not to mention people. The question was where to start. She needed to focus.

Boiling water: that's what she needed. She had

heard a stream a couple miles back, but she wondered if it was safe to leave the dragon alone and unprotected. Looking about, she realized she didn't have a choice, so she silently promised herself as well as the dragon that she would be quick and no harm would come to it, if she could help it.

The walk was fairly long and offered her time to think. She had been traveling aimlessly for days before she encountered the dream dove. When she had left her home, it had been for no other purpose than to be out: out in the world, out of her home and on her feet. The memory of the day she had decided to leave flashed into her mind.

Iviana was standing before the fireplace, amusing her eyes with the dancing flames. It was time to leave. She had been carefully sheltered all her life and now... she could not remain here in this small cottage, all alone, any longer.

Naphtali, her beloved friend and mentor, had recently passed away and the villagers were afraid of Iviana. She had never understood why, but it had always been so. Not only afraid of her, but of her mentor, and what Naphtali was teaching her. But that didn't keep them away when they needed help. The villagers cringed when they saw the vials of liquids foreign to them, when they saw her mentor's collection of needles, the array of herbs. They assumed the two were witches and for all she knew, they were—but Naphtali had simply called it healing and only once did she insist it was not witchcraft. That was enough for Iviana.

There was a method to everything they did. When a child had broken a bone in his forearm, Naphtali sent Iviana to find sticks about the length of the broken arm. They would set the bone straight and form what her mentor had called a "special bandage" around the broken area and, in a few weeks, the arm was healed. The child would smile and run out the door without so much as a thank you and the child's parents would not be heard from unless they needed the "devil's healing" again.

Not even the animals had visited since her mentor's death. Before Naphtali died, they had been the ones to show how grateful they were for the dear lady's help. Those who knew and trusted her would visit daily, weekly, yearly—whenever they could— to pay their respects and to eat what the two had to offer. The fact this was considered strange by others did not enter her mind until her first and last friend visited.

The girl had come for a refill of her mother's healing liquid. The villagers usually did not send children unattended to see the strange lady in the forest cottage, but Naphtali learned the girl's father had left them and her mother was desperate for the medicine. Iviana was eight and the visitor looked to be about her age. Neither girl was shy and they quickly bonded and played while Naphtali prepared the elixir. When various animals came to greet them, the little visitor was delighted, exclaiming she had never been so close to a deer before, except those that had been on her plate. And she couldn't keep from giggling when birds perched on her arms and shoulders. When she received the finished medicine, the little girl excitedly promised to return the next day.

But the promise was not fulfilled the following day, nor was it ever. The people in the village felt they knew better than to allow their children to have anything to do with the wild child who lived with the "cottage witch", as the child was sure to grow into the same. Iviana had lived and grown up quite alone, with very little interaction with anyone but her mentor, aside from the forest animals.

Her dear mentor...

Iviana stifled a sob as she pulled herself out of her thoughts and allowed her eyes to focus on the fireplace once again. Utterly alone, she was afraid she would go mad with it. It was time to get out of this dusty, lifeless house. She could always come back if she found the world too terrible to cope with on her own. She doubted anyone would trouble themselves to rid the world of the "enchanted cottage". They would be too afraid of consequences that would never come.

She turned away from the fireplace and wondered what she should take with her. What would the world ask of her? Pulling a large tote from the basket in the kitchen, she began forming a mental list of what she should bring.

Books: were they practical? Maybe, maybe not, but she could not live without a few in her company. There were three she decided to take. Among them was her mentor's healing diary. It contained everything the woman had ever taught her about healing and then some and would certainly come in handy. Not to mention it would keep her connected with the only person she'd ever loved, and who had ever loved her.

A change of clothes would be in order, a warm cloak, a comb, flint, a knife, jars of preserved fruits and vegetables and ribbons to tie her long, curly hair back. She didn't have a clue what else ought to be packed other than a sturdy blanket. She was certain there would be numerous things she would regret not taking with her, but those items were unknown to her.

Finally, she dressed herself in a comfortable, rustic top and trousers she hoped were suitable for travel, though women did not often wear such things, and slipped her arms through the straps of her pack. Just before opening the door, she remembered the sword her mentor had trained her to use for reasons unknown to her and, after strapping the sword to the belt around her waist, the doorknob turned at her hand's command and everything around her grew silent.

A breeze played over her face and through her long, black-blown hair.

This is it, Iviana thought to herself as it grew harder to breathe. She stepped outside and turned to take one last look at her home. She allowed tears to stream over her face adding to the tear stains that had formed frequently over the last week.

The young woman sighed as she closed the door and glanced about at all the flowers and shrubs that had grown up around the front of the cottage. The fragrant climbing roses waved their farewell in the breeze, encouraging her to continue her journey away from the maddening place—the place where *she had buried her dead alone and the place where she had mourned alone and was left with no comfort but what she could offer herself. Only the thought of leaving had brought her a sort of mysterious comfort. She had always wished to see what was in the world and to see for herself what she had read in books, but could not bear the thought of leaving her elderly mentor on her own.*

Fear, too, had played a part in keeping her in the cottage. Naphtali had never told her why they did not venture into the world outside of their home, but she had always assumed it was because the lady was rather old—though Iviana did not know how old—and that she could not handle what the world held anymore. So why should Iviana assume she, herself, could, even if she was younger and stronger?

These thoughts were no good, however. She was not turning back.

Iviana wiped the tears from her face. The hike back to where the dragon lay had taken longer than she expected and she was disappointed with the amount of water she had managed to carry back in her small, clay bowl. The dragon looked worse than she would have liked and Iviana still had to get a fire lit in order to boil water before she could begin work on the wound.

As she began gathering dry sticks and wasted shrubbery to build a bonfire, the healer realized she hadn't thought to bring a needle. If it was true dragons did not heal well, she doubted the beast would heal without stitches. Oh, if only her mentor were here. Naphtali always knew what to do, it had seemed.

"Naphtali! Where are you?" she shouted to the darkened sky. Tears began to flood her eyes and it grew difficult to breathe. She was irritated that she felt completely lost without her mentor to help her heal this dragon. And she was frustrated Naphtali had not given her more warning.

"Iviana," Naphtali whispered after awakening from another fainting spell. Her voice was small and shaky, her eyelids gray. Iviana knew she was forcing her lungs to inhale and exhale and it was then she realized what was coming. "Sweet, sweet Ivi," the woman continued slowly.

"You're dying," Iviana spoke with a sob, holding her mentor in her arms.

A weak "Yes" followed from Naphtali's lips, but she did not sound afraid; she was relieved.

"Why? What can I do? Tell me what to do!" Iviana cried.

"There's nothing to do. If there were, I would

have done it already."

"You knew this was coming?" Iviana sniffed. "How long have you known?"

Naphtali's breathing grew fainter. "It doesn't matter. Listen, the things I've taught you: don't forget them. Very few..." She struggled to continue. "Very few possess the gift of healing and it must not be lost. Promise me you won't forget."

"Oh, Naphtali." Iviana sobbed and held her head low in anguish and hopelessness. "How can I live without you?"

"Don't speak nonsense." Naphtali continued to struggle, but there was strength in her words. "You'll know very well how to live without me."

"I love you..." Iviana said, "as if you were my own mother."

"I know, sweet daughter." Naphtali closed her eyes, unable to hold them open any longer. "There is something you must know."

Iviana waited for her to continue, afraid she would miss what her teacher wished to say before...

"Your blood... it may be the one precious thing your parents gave you..." Naphtali opened her eyes and forced her hand to reach and gently press against Iviana's face. "Sweet..." Her strength began to fail her.

"Oh, please don't leave me," Iviana cried in anguish.

The elder woman whispered, "I believe... your blood could be enough to..." Her eyes rested on Iviana's face and remained there; her small, thin hand fell to the ground and her tired lungs rested.

Iviana was brought back to the present with the sound of boiling water. She dropped the sticks and turned to find water rolling within the bowl she had left sitting in the dirt.

"How...?" she whispered hoarsely, looking to the dragon for an answer.

It only stared at her without even raising its head. It peered into her eyes, possibly attempting to communicate, but likely not.

Could it really have set the water to boil? she wondered.

Contemplating, she turned her gaze back to the boiling water. It was time to work. She tore a piece of cloth from her blanket and dipped it into the steaming liquid. It stung her hands, but without the sturdy gloves her mentor had provided, she would have to ignore the pain. She was not going to let another living soul die in her hands.

After pressing the hot cloth over the dragon's wound, its eyes darted immediately to observe what she was doing and smoke fluttered from its nostrils. Iviana was half afraid the dragon would become angry from the pain, but it only placed its head on the ground and bore it with smokey nostrils.

When she was finished cleaning the wound, she pulled the knife from her pack and set herself to finding a suitable stick she could carve into a needle. This would be no small chore, for though the dragon's flesh was more tender than she would have supposed, it was still rather leathery.

A needle was one of those things Iviana wished she would have taken with her and she wondered what use Naphtali's diary would be if she did not have the proper tools. It had been a foolish, naive mistake, but it was too late now. The cottage was days behind her.

After selecting the most suitable stick for the job, she began to build the bonfire she had planned to assemble earlier. She would need light for what she was going to do next. Once finished, she pulled the flint from her pack, used it to start the fire and began work on her needle.

The dragon observed her carving, no doubt curious as to what her intent.

"No, dragon, I did not need your help with the fire, thank you." She paused and smiled to herself.

"And yes, this needle is for you."

The dragon blinked and she could not tell if it meant to show its lack of care or if it simply could not understand her.

"Dragon," she began, "I wish you could tell me your name."

It only looked at her, as could now be considered habit.

"I suppose I could name you, like a pet, but I suppose that's rather a foolish idea. You are a great and marvelous dragon, after all, and no one's pet, to be sure."

The dragon closed its eyes, ready to rest, but Iviana continued, "Dragons are very famous, you know, for being monstrous and condescending, leaving the largest and noblest of men feeling insignificant before them. Serves them right, though. They themselves are often very monstrous." She stopped, thinking about those she had met. "But forgive me if I say that you do not seem monstrous at all."

When she finished fashioning the needle, she loosed a long piece of thread from her torn blanket and pulled it through the hole she had carved into the small instrument. When she came near the dragon, with needle in hand, the beast opened its eyes, alarmed by the tiny, pointed thing, a shadow in the firelight.

"Please understand," she said aloud, "this is going to help you. You *will* heal." She nervously patted the upper part of the dragon's belly, offering a bit of comfort before making her first stitch into the dragon's tough flesh. The creature remained tense for the first few stitches, but relaxed after a while, recognizing she worked with experience. From the moment Iviana began, she was in another world: a world where only she and the needle existed. They were working together to create clean and painless stitches and all else faded into the background.

When the last stitch was completed, she tied it off and placed her hand on the dragon, willing it to heal with whatever power she had inside her. She saw the wound glow purple for a moment, as she had often seen happen to Naphtali's patients, but it was only a small instant, so she always assumed it was her imagination. Still, Naphtali had always said placing her hand on the ailment was vital to the healing process and never to be forgotten.

∽

The next morning, Iviana awoke propped against the dragon. She couldn't recall falling asleep, but was grateful the dragon didn't seem to mind.

She examined the gash she had closed the night before, thankful it wasn't infected, but could only hope her observations were correct. How would an infected wound appear on a dragon? She looked to the dragon's face.

He was watching her.

Yes, *it* was a *he*. She was certain.

Her stomach growled.

"Well, if I'm hungry, I'm certain your large stomach is starving," she said, wandering off.

Iviana returned a while later with a small hare for herself and a half dozen or so various critters for the dragon.

"I'm sorry," she said. "I don't know what you eat... or how much, but I suppose this is a start."

She laid the animals before the dragon who pushed himself up with his front legs and glared down at the pile. He raised a brow bone in disgust.

"I'm sorry," Iviana apologized again. "Do you... do you eat cooked meat?" The young woman supposed it could be possible, as she was fairly certain he had boiled the water for her the night before.

She prepared the bonfire and, as she reached for the flint in her pack, a flame appeared in the pit.

"Show off," she muttered, preparing the meat for cooking.

Beginning with a squirrel, she roasted the critter along with her own and then laid it before the dragon who nudged it away with his muzzle.

"Not for you? Fine, it'll be my breakfast."

Next she laid the hare she had planned to eat before him. He didn't push it away, but he didn't eat it either.

"Well, that was a waste. What *do* you want?"

The dragon rose slowly and moved to a patch of what looked like red aloe—though, in this foreign area, she couldn't be certain—and stole a bite from it. The dragon glanced back at her as he chewed.

"Ah, a vegetarian," Iviana commented. "Here I was afraid it was my cooking."

∞ 3 ∞

IVIANA FOUND HERSELF in a village livelier than she had ever seen. When she had traveled through the village near her home, it had been a quiet place where the villagers mostly kept to themselves. Here, there were carts everywhere with folk shouting their merchandise was the best in all Kierelia.

Hanging from building to building were colorful, decorative ribbons; children were playing games in the streets and stands overflowed with a bright array of sweet smelling fruits and vegetables for sale. Carts dripping with trinkets such as hairclasps, earrings, bracelets and necklaces were displayed and though these trifles were pretty, they failed to capture Iviana's interest. She had grown up without such items and did not understand their value.

Across the way, she heard a man with a long beard and large belly in baggy brown garb shouting, "The end is near! Doomsday is at hand!"

Iviana giggled, for, despite these warnings, the atmosphere remained festive and she felt her walls tumbling down. Any inhibitions she had toward strangers began to disintegrate.

Behind her, a horse whinnied and she turned in time to see the animal rear up on hind legs, nearly throwing its rider.

"Oy! Watch where you're going, girly!" the rider shouted roughly.

This sobered her. She resolved to find what was needed and leave the town as quickly as possible.

It was some sort of paste, she was after, for her mentor's diary. She had noticed while reading through it that morning that the binding was beginning to come loose and she didn't have an understanding of how to sew it back, nor did she have a proper needle with which to do so.

She wondered what Naphtali would have done with the diary. *Most likely she'd have known how to mend it herself,* she guessed.

Having left the dragon in the dry clearing many miles back, Iviana had promised she would return shortly and asked that he not leave until she had returned. He hadn't agreed, but he hadn't disagreed either. In truth, he had only stared and she hoped that didn't mean he thought she was foolish for trying to ask such a thing of a dragon.

Pushing her way through the crowds of the main street, she spotted a large sign displaying the image of a book and hoped the shop might have something for her.

Once within, Iviana's breath was quite taken away by the multitude of shelves packed full of colorful books in all shapes, sizes and bindings. It was a beautiful scene and Iviana wished she could remain for a while, but her dragon was waiting for her, she was sure, and he might begin to worry about her. She chuckled at the idea, but thought, *Perhaps.*

After walking to the end of the shop, Iviana looked about, but could not find a shopkeeper.

She called out curiously, "Hello?"

No answer.

"I could use some advice on how to repair a book," she called again, finishing with, "A paste would suit..."

Still silence followed.

Iviana sighed. She supposed it wouldn't hurt to look around for a little while. There were many books she would have liked to purchase, but she realized then that the shopkeeper would probably expect some kind of payment or trade and she doubted she had anything to trade. A lack of money was definite. Villagers who had received healing from her and Naphtali had always insisted on some sort of payment, afraid that, without it, the "witches" would curse them. But it was usually things the women had very little use for—like money. Now she wished she would have thought to take the little jar filled with the "unneeded" currency with her: another naive mistake.

She was about to leave when she heard humming coming from a slightly open door in the back of the large shop. Knowing full well that what she was doing was considered bad manners, she walked to the back of the store and stepped through the door, expecting to discover the source of the tune. Instead, she found herself outdoors in a green, roughly fenced yard with a small, rugged shack in the far corner. Still, there was no one in sight.

Iviana heard the humming again until it turned to singing. It seemed to be coming from the little shack at the end of the yard, so, swiftly and silently, she made her way over and peeked through the entryway. What she found astonished her, for the little building was full of birds: a great many of all sorts, including some she had never seen before. The woman dancing, singing and casting seed about for the fluttery animals to nibble up surprised her more than the collection of exotic birds. Her long brown, slightly grayed locks were dreaded and embellished with feathers and her baggy drapes in rich, surly brown, twirled around her as she went. She, with her wild hair and clothes and her dancing was a sight Iviana had never beheld.

Iviana assumed the woman was unaware of her presence until the lady sang, "Coome, cooome, come in, curious girl. Don't be shy!" When Iviana did not move, the woman stopped her dancing and turned to Iviana. "I mean it; come in. You can help me feed my *darlings*," she cooed as she went back to casting seed upon the birds.

Iviana shyly entered the little room and accepted the handful of seed the singing woman offered. "Just hold out your hand like this." She shoved Iviana's arm into the air then dared the birds with a raised eyebrow. "We'll see who's bold enough to feed from the stranger's hand."

The peculiar woman continued casting seed while Iviana waited with her hand outstretched. Eventually, a little red bird flew into her palm and began pecking at the seed. Then another joined.

Several more came and perched on her arms, shoulders and head, as if waiting their turn to be fed by the stranger.

Facing the opposite direction, the woman spoke, "That's what I thought. I just knew they'd like you. You have the *way* about you."

"The way?" Iviana inquired.

"Oh, you know," the woman dismissed the question. "Now, don't tell me! Let me guess it... Rackell? No, no, no... Marie? No, I suppose not. Well, you had better tell me."

"My name?" Iviana asked. "It's Ivi."

"Ivianaaa, yes. I've heard about you, but you prefer Ivi, I see. Well, then we'll have it your way, Ivi. I'm Bell. Spelled like the bell you ring. That's why I like to *riiiing and sing, ring and sing*." She sang the last.

"How did you hear of me, ma'am?" Iviana asked, utterly bewildered.

"Ooh, please, no 'ma'am'. I just told you my name. May as well make use of the knowledge."

"I'm sorry. Bell." Iviana submitted.

"Wonderful! Now tell me, what has brought you to my birdhouse?"

Iviana shifted her weight, causing a few startled birds to fly from her head and shoulders over to

33

Bell's. "I'm looking for something to mend the binding of a book."

Bell looked at Iviana as though she were a wild thing. "So you came looking in my bird house? Really, dear, not very clever of you, is it?" she scolded softly.

Iviana stifled a giggle. "No, I saw the bookshop and I thought perhaps..."

"Oooh, of course, of course. I always forget that's there. Did you find what you were looking for?"

"N-no... that's how I came to find you here. I was looking for the owner."

"Ah, well, unfortunately that would be me. Troublesome thing, that store. I like to forget about it."

Iviana was a little astonished by this strange woman, but at the same time, Bell had a warm nature that put her at ease.

A white flash darted through the door just then—startling Iviana—and gracefully perched itself on Bell's shoulder.

"Aah, I wondered if you would come by. She's as lovely as you said she was," Bell commented to the dove.

Iviana looked closer and realized it was the same

dove she had tried to follow the day before. "I know that dove," she said a little hoarsely.

"Mhmmm, he's the one who told me about you," Bell said. Then she paused and tilted her head as though listening to something. She nodded. "I agree, but there's so much baggage there." She gestured at Iviana and listened another moment before adding with a sigh, "I suppose. You're never wrong."

Iviana interrupted with, "Can you really understand it?"

"*Him*, dear, for heaven's sake. Of course I can. You have no idea who this is, do you?"

Iviana uncomfortably changed weight from one foot to the other. "Er, no... I don't."

"Well." Bell looked her up and down. "I've a feeling you will one day." She returned her attention to the dove and spoke. "Of course. Thank you and come back soon. You know I'd be terribly lonesome without you." With that, the dove turned his head to Iviana and seemed to nod before fluttering away.

Bell sighed and knelt down to pet one of the birds and continued her previous song.

Iviana wondered if Bell had forgotten she was there. Edging toward the door, she muttered, "I suppose I should be going."

Bell rose and walked herself out of the shack, leaving Iviana blinking after her.

Suddenly the older woman peeked her head back inside the door and asked, "You coming, girly?"

Iviana blinked once more and followed Bell into the bookstore.

All the while, Bell continued to sing:

> *"You long for silence*
> *to release noise as thunder,*
> *But, darling, you know,*
> *you have Him forever."*

She turned to face Iviana just as they stepped through the door, "You do know that don't you?"

Iviana was puzzled. "Know what?"

"That you're never alone. Never ever. He is with you, always."

"Who??" Iviana muttered, bewildered.

"*Oh,* you know... Now, where is that vial?" She was rummaging through a desk piled high with maps, mittens, feathers...

"I *don't* know, though–" Iviana tried to insist.

"Aaah, *here* it is!" Bell held up a small vial with an icky brown liquid in it.

"What is that?" Iviana asked, attempting to mask

her disgust.

"It's for your book. I've a feeling the thing may never fall to pieces with this stuff holding it." She placed it in the girl's hands.

"Why, thank you. Thank you very much, but how shall I pay you?"

"Oooh, that's a good question! Let me see..." Bell scratched the surface of her head. "I know!" She walked over to where the books sat on shelf upon shelf and began rummaging through them. "There you are." She pulled a large, slightly beaten book from the shelf and held it before Iviana. "You can take this old thing off my hands. I've no room to spare for it."

"But I don't think that's how it works," Iviana insisted. "Shouldn't I trade you something for it?"

"You are! You're trading me the space for the vial. Unless you would prefer something else? Really, I thought you would be happy to help me, but if the book doesn't suit—"

"No! Thank you for... the trade... and the book," Iviana smiled at the warm woman, despite how thunderstruck she felt by the meeting.

"Don't thank me, girly. You're doing *me* the favor. This place is a mess and I've got to make space for more, don't you think? Now, you'd best be off, but I've got to tell you something before you go. It's a message. Let me think, what *was* it? Ah, yes, I already told you. Well, thank heaven for that!"

Iviana longed to ask what it was, but Bell began shooing her out the door. "My, isn't it late? Well, you'll make it before dark. Listen here, mind you don't take the main road through the forest."

"Why not?" Iviana asked, though she felt she already knew what the answer would be.

"Oh, you know... Now, off with you." The woman slammed the door closed before Iviana could respond.

"Well," Iviana said to herself, "that was certainly intriguing. Too bad the main road's the swiftest route..."

ᚹ

Walking along the main path through the forest, a shadow appeared at Iviana's side. She wished she hadn't allowed herself to become so consumed by her thoughts of the eccentric Bell when she should have been paying attention to her surroundings. Sneaking a quick peek over her shoulder, it was confirmed she was being closely followed by a group of five men. They were not gentlemen from the looks of them. Iviana picked up her pace, hoping to come upon other travelers on the road.

"Oy, sweetie!" a gruff voice called to her. "Where ye goin' to so fast? Ain't nuffin 'ere'bouts but us."

The men snickered and set their pace to hers.

Why couldn't I have just listened *to Bell?* Iviana scolded herself. She was at a complete loss for what to do. She couldn't run—they'd surely catch her. She could turn and fight, but five against one? The odds weren't good and she had never entered into actual combat with her weapon before, aside from the man who wanted her dragon's heart, but he had been merciful.

Help me, she pleaded. To whom, she couldn't say.

The next moment, a large man leaped for Iviana and grabbed her by the arms, yanking them behind her back before she could attempt to snatch her sword.

He held her too tightly and a sudden anger arose within Iviana inspiring her to roar through gritted teeth, "You may not have me. I demand that you let me go!"

The man who had called to her earlier stood

before her now and blinked a moment in surprise before grabbing at her hair and pulling. "There, there, pretty lioness," he cooed with a smirk. "It ain't any good to 'ave a temper wiv us. We don't bite."

She blew a piece of loose hair out of her face and muttered, "I suppose I do."

With that she elbowed the man holding her arms, pulled out her sword and chopped off the arm that had been jerking at her hair. The man looked down and screamed as the others stood watching, too stunned to move. The man with one arm continued screaming and the one who had been elbowed knelt, buckled over, on the ground. He shouted through the pain, "Don't just stand there, you muggins; make her *pay!*"

Two men awoke from their daze and started toward her, but Iviana was prepared this time. She held her weapon out, ready to defend herself.

A short, skinny man pulled out a hand knife. "Steady there, little fool," he said, "if ye settle yerself now, Big Han might 'ave mercy on ye an' let ye live. Ye could travel wiv us, hey?"

When he was finished speaking, he lunged toward her with his knife, but she tossed it aside and out of his hand with her sword. At the same moment, however, the man grabbed at her wrists, forcing the sword from the hand that held it. He worked to knock her to the ground calling to the other man to get the ropes ready. Iviana struggled with him and, though he was skinny, it was apparent whatever he did for a living kept him in shape. The man with the ropes, along with another man, grabbed her ankles and attempted to bind them together. She dropped to the ground cursing and roaring at the men who, now that they were in control again, only laughed.

"There, darlin'," the skinny man said, "save it for Big H-" The skinny man never finished his sentence. His eyes rolled back and he dropped to the ground, a knife in his back.

Iviana searched for the source of the knife and discovered it had flown from the hand of the man who had tried to take her dragon's life the day before. He had proven to be a good fighter then and he did so now as two of the men left her to take on the stranger. He fought them both at once and took one down within the first moments of battle.

Iviana turned her attention from them and strove to think of a way to take care of the man she had elbowed, who was now attempting to tie her wrists together. She knew if she let him finish his knots, she would be totally helpless. Not knowing what else to do, and hoping she was physically capable of what she was going to attempt, Iviana heaved her tied up feet over her head and knocked the large man square in the jaw. He swore and reached for his knife as she dove for her sword. Lying on the ground, she rolled and swung her sword into the air, meeting the man's drawn blade as it was coming down on her. He continued thrashing the air over her, but she met his every attempt, somehow managing to wriggle herself backward. This continued until she backed too far and struck her head against the trunk of a tree. The man went in for the killer blow, but she rolled in time. Forcing the man off-balance, he fell to the ground with his attempt. When he propelled himself onto his back, she was kneeling over him, sword ready.

"Give me a reason not to kill you," she dared him.

The man only offered a faint smirk and admitted huskily, "Too late, lass." A faint bit of blood gleamed from his lower lip before his eyes went still. Iviana rolled him over and found he'd managed to stab himself with his own blade in the chaos of his fall.

Though she despised watching another death occur before her eyes, Iviana admitted she was glad to be rid of the man and, after cutting through the ropes around her ankles, she turned to find that the would-be-dragon-slayer had frightened off his opponent, who was running into the woods along with the one-handed fellow.

Speaking to the back that faced her, she declared, "I'm not some helpless damsel who needs rescuing, you know."

He didn't speak or even turn around.

"What are you doing here, anyway?" she demanded. "Are you following me?"

The man gave a short, harsh laugh and strolled into the woods.

"Hey," she called and followed after him.

He continued walking, but responded, "I have nothing to say to you, except... why can't you just accept help when you were obviously in need of some? And maybe you could try a little gratitude."

"Alright, thank you, man who nearly killed my beautiful dragon," Iviana responded stubbornly.

The man turned his gaze on her and replied in an exasperated tone, "See? This is why I don't care to waste my time speaking with you, so why don't you get back to rescuing dragons and slaying damsels or whatever it is you do."

Iviana ceased following him as he continued his trek through the forest, but a nasty twinge of guilt struck her. No one had forced him to help her. It would have been easy enough to ignore her situation.

She sighed, ran in the direction she had seen him go and caught him just as he swung a leg over the back of a horse.

"Wait!" she called, but he ignored her and encouraged his horse into a trot. "Wait!" She yelled again, but the horse moved into a canter. "Thank you!" she shouted toward his disappearing frame.

☙ 4 ❧

IVIANA GREETED THE beast with a smile as she entered the rocky clearing. She was grateful he hadn't left. "You have no idea what a full day I've had." He stared at her as though waiting for an explanation. "Oh, not just yet," she insisted, relieving herself of her pack. "I'm starving. I'll be back with my dinner in a bit. You can take care of yourself a little longer?"

He glared at her, obviously offended by the question.

"I'm only teasing," she assured him and offered a pat on the back.

When Iviana returned from her hunt, she started a fire and set her food to cook.

"I hope you don't mind if *I* continue to enjoy meat. It's a tough habit to break."

The dragon ignored her.

"Well, do you want to hear about my day?"

The beast responded by turning about to face her and curling up a few feet away.

"I... came across that man who tried to kill you yesterday." She waited for a response, but did not receive one. "In his defense, he did spare your life and he saved mine today, but I'd rather not get into that. Lets see... Oh! I was able to obtain a paste for Naphtali's diary." She pulled the vial from her pack and turned it about in her hands. "The woman who gave it to me, she was sort of... incredible, in a way. I haven't met many people, but I've certainly never met anyone like her."

Iviana proceeded to pull the diary from her bag and worked on mending it. When she was finished, it held as impressively as Bell had promised and she was grateful for her chance meeting with the lady. At random, she opened the diary and proceeded to read aloud from one of the last entries,

"I regret to inform these tattered pages that I am ill and cannot find a cure in this realm. I have tried the door in Jaela's Cavern, but it is no use. Its golden face taunts me and the voice of my kin is like ice to my heart. Yet I could manage all this without complaint if only I knew my sweetest Ivi would be alright. If only there were someone for her. Dearest One, watch over her and guide her in her destiny."

Iviana sat, confused and stunned by what she had read, wondering who this "Dearest One" was and why Naphtali would write to them in her diary... about *her*.

When she looked up, the dragon had moved less than a foot from her face with his head peering down as though trying to view the pages. He gazed into her bright blue eyes, trying to penetrate some knowledge into her mind.

"What is it?" she asked him anxiously.

He nudged the book with his muzzle and she assumed he expected her to read it again. She obeyed.

"...I have tried the door at Jaela's Cavern, but it is no–"

When she came to these words, the dragon blew hot air into her face.

Iviana couldn't keep her heart from pounding as excitement began to bubble within her. "Do you know what she's referring to, dragon? Do you know this door with the..." she glanced into the book for the words she sought, "'golden face?'"

More hot air blew into her face and the dragon floated away, crouched down and motioned for her to perch herself on his back.

"You can take me there?" she asked him, barely

able to conceive his ardor or how quickly he had healed from the wound he had received only the day before.

He crouched lower and waited.

Iviana *wanted* to leap onto his back and let him fly her away to wherever he wished to go, but she realized their were other factors she needed to consider. "Alright," she said to him. "I would like to go with you, but since you probably can't tell me how far we're going, will you allow me to fetch a few supplies?"

The dragon glared a while, then slowly sat himself upright, looking annoyed and anxious.

"I'll hurry," she promised and nabbed what she had prepared for dinner, resolved to trade it in town for food that could sustain a journey on back of a dragon.

೫ 5 ೫

IT WAS DARK and Iviana thought it best to return to her dragon before he grew anxious. She knew this continued consideration for his nervous system was foolish, but she could not help feeling her thinking was correct. So, she quickly made her way to the edge of the town. Ready to sprint toward the woods, she was startled by the pain-filled grunt that sounded from around the corner of a nearby building.

Nervously, she crept over to where the sound had come and spied *him*: the-would-be-dragon-slayer. It occurred to her their running into one another was peculiar, but she focused on the issue at hand. He was surrounded by a group of ten or so unbelievably grotesque men and appeared to have been rendered unconscious. As the group busied themselves with the chore of tying him up, Iviana scanned the area and located a horse-drawn wagon she assumed the ugly men had procured to haul their heavy captive. She listened for any hint of where they planned to take him, but heard ramblings about their empty stomachs instead.

What in the world has he done to warrant an abduction by such a group of men? Iviana wondered a little apprehensively. Whatever the reason, it was not going to keep her from trying to help him. She owed him and she knew it. The question was, what could she possibly do? She was one woman; she had no friends and from what she had gathered while trading in the town, it was doubtful the local authorities would be willing to aid her.

Iviana watched as they shoved her would-be-dragon-slayer into the wagon and mounted several of the horses surrounding. It was apparent every one of the men would be acting as "escort."

Unable to hatch a better plan, Iviana pursued the group for some time and was near collapsing from fatigue when the repulsive men resolved to rest for the night. Drained as she was, Iviana hoped she would be able to steal up to the wagon while they slept, but was thwarted when she overheard their raspy voices discuss who would take the first lookout.

These men genuinely plan to protect their prize,

Iviana realized, perplexed by the knowledge.

She concluded she would have to wait and hope the lookouts would fall asleep. However, without realizing it, the young woman, herself, fell into slumber.

The sleeping traveler awoke to the sound of wings settling in the space before her. When a shadow fell over her frame, she hoped before daring to open her eyes that it was her dragon—that he had found her somehow. When at last she lifted her eyelids, Iviana was relieved to discover her anticipation had not been in vain. Without further thought, she leaped to her booted feet and embraced the dragon. Though, of course, once she realized she was coddling a fierce, glorious, even dangerous beast, she immediately retreated, abashed at her thoughtless action. The beast did not mind, however, and only gazed at her, or into her. Whichever it was, his regard was uncanny.

Iviana remembered what she'd been preoccupied with the evening before and scolded herself for having fallen asleep. A man's life might be in danger. How was she going to find him now? She was certainly no tracker.

After examining the campsite, there appeared to be enough of an imprint from the wagon wheels that it would be easy enough to follow, even for her. Perhaps, if she and the dragon hurried, they'd catch up with the abductors before they had a chance to harm the mysterious man.

The dragon, gathering she wished to follow the trail, crouched low as he had the day before. This time, Iviana did not hesitate. Instead, she hoisted herself onto his back and concluded she fit quite comfortably into the furrows of his back, almost as if they had been made for her.

Iviana proceeded to inform him of who they were after. "I know you owe him nothing, but I do. And after all, he never actually *killed* you..."

Atop the dragon, she had no way of seeing the creature roll his eyes as he began to pump his large wings, swirling foliage about and launching his body into the air. The dragon's companion suffered some vertigo in the sudden rush of their lift-off, but was filled with breathless wonder at sight of the treetops below her. Her anticipation only grew when they had cleared the woods, for she could feel him readying to jettison forward. It was a rush of excitement as his sinewy wings caught the natural breezes of the day and the pair soared forward, higher and faster than Iviana had ever traveled before. It was an occurrence she knew she would never forget: the sensation of traveling above the ground, above the trees and near the clouds, where everything below was so very small. It was unmatchable, she was certain.

The wild-haired maiden spread her arms out as though they were wings and breathed. "So *this* is flying," she uttered in a peaceful sigh.

It was some time before the party appeared in view. So long as she and her dragon remained unseen, Iviana hoped this would be fairly simple. The difficult part would be communicating her plan to the dragon. Though it ought to be fairly uncomplicated, she wasn't certain the dragon ever actually understood what she spoke to him. Nevertheless, before she could attempt to communicate it, the dragon slowly urged himself closer, keeping his shadow always behind the travelers, and she soon wondered if he shared her thoughts.

Then, without warning, he swiftly swooped down and plucked the man from the wagon with his hind legs, then flashed a few hundred feet into the sky. Iviana was nearly flung from the dragon's back before she realized what was happening. But it was obvious the men below had not been afforded time either, for not an arrow flew their way.

"Who knew you were so clever?" she praised him proudly.

She was basking in the glory of the flight when a voice below broke through the silence of the sky.

"Is that the dragon-savior, I hear?"

Iviana stifled a laugh as she pictured the man uncomfortably dangling from her dragon's talons. "Ay, and you're lucky I've taken up the occupation or you'd be who knows where by now," she called out.

"Touche!" was his reply. "May I ask to whom I am so indebted?"

"I haven't named the dragon."

The man hiccuped a short laugh. "I was referring to you, my lady."

My lady? She'd never been addressed that way before. Always it had been "girl" or behind her back "witch" and "little devil".

"Iviana," she called out.

"Ivi, lovely to meet you. I'm Flynn."

"Charmed," she responded just before the dragon gracefully floated into an opening in the woods and dumped his cargo. It took Iviana a while to untie the dreadful knots the men had used to en-bondage Flynn, but after some time, she succeeded in freeing him.

"That was one of the most terrifying experiences of my life," he commented upon his freedom.

"Why did they take you? What did they want?"

"Honestly, I don't know," was his genuine reply, "but I was referring to the flying."

"Oh, you should have tried my view. It was grand."

"I believe it, but how did you come upon me? Were you following me?" Flynn asked her with a smirk.

Iviana replied with a smirk to match, "Yes. After I saw you abducted from the village inn, I decided to try rescuing damsels for a change."

"Mm, how is it?"

"Irritating."

"I know the feeling. Tried it once, no good."

Iviana smiled as she realized to whom he was referring. "You really don't know why all those men knocked you out, tied you up and heavily guarded you?"

Flynn thought a while then answered, "I'm not positive as to why they wanted me, but I do have an idea as to why there were so many."

"And?"

"I have a reputation," he said with an ornery grin.

Iviana raised a brow. "I'm sure."

Flynn chuckled easily, then said, "Well, I thank you both a thousand times over for your help and I'd love to stay and chat with the savior of dragons and damsels, but I'm afraid I've an appointment elsewhere, so.."—he started into the woods—"it was lovely meeting you."

"What appointment?" Iviana prodded.

He hesitated and the playfulness that had made up his person vanished as he said, "It's the reason I wanted the dragon's heart, I'm afraid." He looked uncomfortably at the beast. "The creature to whom I now owe my life."

"But why?"

He sighed and took a seat upon the ground, leaning his back against a tree. "My sister is the appointment."

When he didn't continue, Iviana coaxed him again."Go on. Please?"

Flynn hesitated, then stood and said, "It's nothing." Before she knew it, he'd trudged into the woods again.

"It's definitely not nothing, Flynn. Whatever it is, it's apart of your life and I'd like to hear it," she called to him with stubborn compassion.

He paused and called back, "Ay, my lady. It's my

life."

She took the hint as a bit of a blow, but wasn't going to give in that easily. "Tell me what you want with my dragon's heart," she demanded.

He halted, sighed, but then returned to her and explained, "My sister is dying; possibly already dead. I've searched every nearby village, begging people for their help, but none want to risk catching whatever it is she has and, lets face it, none of them would know what to do about it anyway." He stopped, looking self-conscious, but she nodded for him to continue. "I promised a witch the heart of a dragon if she would remove the illness from my sister. It's the only hope I have... or *had*."

"Your sister's alone?"

He was surprised by her reaction to what he had just told her. Anyone else would have spat at him for associating with a witch. "No. I've hired a woman to stay with her. I'm know she's doing what she can, but it's not much. And now I've got to get back to her, Ivi. Goodbye."

Flynn turned to go, but Iviana interrupted. "Would you *stop* walking away every time we meet?"

He turned back to her. "What would you have me do?" he asked simply.

Iviana thought a moment, contemplating

whether or not she was brave enough to take on what she was about to offer. "I may be able to help her."

Flynn looked surprised. "You're a witch?"

"No. A healer. It's hard to explain. In fact, I can't really…"

He took her hand and with glistening eyes spoke urgently, "You really think you can help her?"

Iviana closed her eyes and checked within herself before answering, "I can't promise. I'm not my mentor."

"Then lets go; we can't afford to waste more time." He hustled into the woods.

"Uh," she called, "want to take the dragon?"

His face grew brighter. "Yes."

∞6∞

THOUGH THEY WERE forced to be extra
cautious in order to avoid being spotted by dragon-
hunters, the journey that would have occupied
several days on foot spanned the time of only a few
hours by flight. The sights they flew over tickled
Iviana immensely, for all that she saw was foreign to
her and everything appeared unusual from the view
of a dragon. She squealed over little winding roads,
tiny trees and a small number of tiny people. Flynn
was highly amused by the surprising sounds coming
from Iviana; he never would have believed it of the
stubborn swords-woman if he hadn't heard it
himself.

"You should really get out more," he teased.

"Sorry! This is all *new* to me. I've only known
my dragon since the day you tried to kill him."

"When did the grand beast become your dragon?

Maybe you're his human."

"Suits me fine," she replied with a smirk.

Finally, they flew over a small, still village with just a handful of rugged homes.

"That's us," Flynn informed. "Where do we leave the dragon?"

"I think we ought to have him drop us in the woods so he can decide where he wants to go. He'll find me if I need him, I think."

The dragon agreed, landing in a lush green area of the forest near the village, but seemed uncomfortable when Iviana prepared to leave him, releasing tiny wisps of smoke from his nose.

She stepped over to him and petted his muzzle. "I know. We were to visit that Jaela's Cavern weren't we? We will, I promise. I've got to see to this and I'll return to you as soon as I'm able, alright?"

The dragon stared fixedly into her eyes with his beautiful deep green ones, relaying that he was going to trust her promise—or so Iviana guessed—and the curls of smoke ceased. Iviana turned to say something to Flynn and when she looked back to her dragon, he had vanished. Flynn raised his eyebrows, shrugged and urged her to follow him.

Once they reached the village, Flynn led the way to a dwarfish house at the end of the tiny development and rushed inside without a word. Iviana invited herself in.

It was much cozier on the inside than it appeared outwardly, with a fluffy sofa, wooden chairs with pillows and flowery curtains that hung open before a large set of windows. They were being lightly tossed by a fresh-scented breeze just like the curtains in her home used to.

Iviana heard voices coming from a room beside the entry to the kitchen and moved herself that way. She lightly knocked upon the open door before taking a step inside.

Flynn, who was sitting on a bed holding the hand of a girl who looked to be in her teens, glanced to where Iviana was in the doorway and spoke cheerfully, "Here she is, Laurel; this is Ivi." He motioned for Iviana to come nearer. "She's going to see what she can do for you."

The barely conscious Laurel looked into Iviana's eyes and softly murmured, "Thank you, Ivi." The girl was drenched with sweat, but shivered as though she were chilled to the bone. An aged woman standing in the corner informed Iviana that Laurel had not been able to keep food or drink down for several days.

"Alright," Iviana said. "If I could have a little

space, please. Would it be alright if we put out the fire? I could also use a few cold, wet rags; if I could be shown where to find these, I'll gladly fetch them myself."

"Put out the fire?" the elder woman spoke worriedly. "She's freezing as it is."

"We will keep her covered, but as I'm certain she's in enough discomfort as it is, the cold in the room will hardly make any difference. You will fetch me the rags, please."

The older lady stood over her patient and was nearly brought to tears.

"Good woman," Iviana snapped at her, "now."

Iviana did not wish to be brusque, but knew the sooner she was able to focus and begin treating the girl, the better Laurel's chances were of recovering; she did not need to have anyone about who would second guess her. Naphtali had taught her it would only make matters worse and divide her concentration.

After Flynn finished putting out the fire, Iviana informed him she was going out to find herbs for the healing and asked if he would stay by the girl's side until her return.

Flynn followed her out of the room. "Is there any chance, Ivi? You're not just pretending for her benefit? I need to know the truth."

Iviana gritted her teeth. "You mustn't be negative, Flynn. There is hope and I will do what must be done. Place the cool rags on her forehead, arms and chest when they are brought to you. When I get back, you will need to leave the room. Do you understand?"

Flynn lowered his eyes to the floor and nodded.

"Go to her. She needs your comfort; it will do her good. Speak *positively.*"

When Iviana returned with the herbs, Flynn and the caregiver left the room as instructed by Iviana. With all distractions diminished, she proceeded in readying what was needed and encouraged the girl. Naphtali had always pressed how important this was. *"Speak life, Ivi, and it is what you will get."*

"Your brother cares a great deal for you, Laurel."

The girl smiled sleepily.

"And your caregiver; what is her name? Can you tell me?"

"Mariah. She is sweet to me."

"It's nice to have a sweet companion. They are your ally in battle and your comfort in defeat... your teacher..." Iviana shook her head, ridding herself of memories. "Drink this. I know it smells, but it will be worth it, I promise."

"What if I can't keep it down?"

"You will. I'll make sure of it." Iviana smiled reassuringly.

Soon after, the girl drifted into a restful sleep and Iviana touched her hand to the girl's fevered head, pressing her healing into it and urging her body to keep the mixture down. The hint of violet glowed beneath her hand, then flashed out of existence as it always did. Iviana shrugged and opened a window. It was a cool night and the fresh air would rejuvenate her patient.

Hours later, Flynn entered the room, waking Iviana from where she knelt by the bed with her head resting on the mattress.

"Is she dying?" he asked, his face a mess of worry.

"No, Flynn."

"She's so still. Oh, she must be." He pressed his palms to his eyes. "I can't stand this waiting. Just tell me the truth of it now. I don't want to hear it when it's too late."

"Flynn, don't you utter another word, " Iviana snapped and stood to her feet ready to bite the man's ears off, but Laurel began to moan in her bed. "That's not right," she muttered, feeling the girl's forehead. "Her fever was nearly gone just a little while ago." Tearing the rags off the girl, she called to the caregiver who was sitting up in the next room, "Bring a bowl of cold water."

Flynn groaned. "Ooh, I knew it..." He was near tears, but Iviana grabbed him by the shoulders and shook him.

"Stop it, Flynn. Just stop it. If this girl does not live—though I can assure you she will—but if she doesn't, you will have nothing to blame but your own stupid words. Be positive and that is what you'll get. Speak life and you will have it, in this case at least."

Flynn stared into Iviana's icy blue eyes. "Forgive me," he consented. "How can I help you?"

"Leave," she answered and turned to prepare whatever herbs were left.

By morning, Laurel was soundly sleeping, her fever broken. Flynn and Mariah were tripping over themselves, eager to serve the young woman who had brought the miracle about, but Iviana continued to request that they leave the room, assuring them all she needed was quiet and a good book. At that, they scrambled to find her one, but she insisted she had her own.

Laurel slept restfully through most of the day, waking only to sip a little broth: the first sustenance she had been able to keep down in a long time. The poor thing had been so frail when Iviana first saw her, but over the course of the next few days, Iviana saw to it she was fattened, and quickly. She did not want even the slightest chance the girl would relapse and so strove to give her what strength she could provide. Therefore, nasty green mixtures continued until the girl begged that they would not. Iviana consented only when Laurel was on her feet again.

On that day, a humble feast was prepared in honor of the healer and former invalid. The four sat around a table together for the first time since Iviana had been there and she realized later that it was one of the most enjoyable evenings she had ever spent. Formerly, she'd never eaten with anyone but Naphtali and her dragon—who she had been visiting regularly during her stay—and all this company at once warmed her heart to its center.

Laurel raised her cup. "To my dear healer and friend!" she said.

Flynn and Mariah raised their glasses as well and Flynn added, "To the lady who fought for my little Laurel's healing when I had lost hope..."

They tapped their glasses together, causing Iviana to blush and wave her hands at them in embarrassment while she fought back tears. Never had she been so thanked or had so many smiling faces turned upon her.

"I don't know how I came to be here tonight," Iviana began quietly, "but I am very grateful that I am able to share this meal with you all."

The three disagreed with her, however, insisting that they were the ones who were grateful and honored by her company. Iviana begged that the subject be changed.

"How did you meet our Iviana, Flynn?" Laurel asked.

Flynn looked directly at his sister and was completely at a loss for words. He didn't know how to explain his hunt for a dragon without mentioning his pact with the witch.

"We were after the same... prey, I'm afraid." Iviana answered. "I can't say that I won it fairly, but your brother was gracious enough to resign it to me."

"Oh, bravo, Flynn!" Laurel cheered him. "Always so kind and courteous; that is why we adore you."

Mariah insisted they toast to that as well. Flynn cast a mortified expression upon Iviana.

Later that night, Iviana agreed to take a walk with Flynn and the air was as fresh and cool as it had been on her first night there.

"Thank you for, uh, covering for me," Flynn said

a little meekly.

Iviana chuckled. "It wasn't so hard. What I spoke was true and their reaction warranted. It was good of you not to heartlessly take my dragon from me."

He chuckled halfheartedly and shrugged.

"Why did you spare the dragon that day..." Iviana began, "if you were so desperate for Laurel's sake?"

"I suppose it was your conviction. It was life or death for you, though it was the dragon at stake and not your own life. It didn't feel right, anyway, with it just lying there, defenseless, save you. Speaking of, have you checked up on the beast lately?"

Iviana nodded. "Yes. He's getting restless."

They were silent a while as they strolled into the woods behind the house.

Flynn asked pensively after a time, "You'll want to be leaving soon then?"

"Yes."

"Where will you go?"

"I read something about a... a door in a place called Jaela's Cavern. My dragon seems to know where it is and is adamant we go. That's why I was in the village the night those men took you. We needed supplies."

Flynn shook his head. "Well, you're certainly full

of mysteries... but I hope you'll stay with us a short while, at least. I know Laurel will want to learn everything she can about you." He raised an eyebrow. "I believe I overheard her asking Mariah if she thought you had magic."

Iviana laughed. "Oh, dear, I'd rather she not get that impression."

Flynn chuckled with her and bent down to pull a small plant from the ground. "Is this what you used to help her heal?"

She nodded.

"Miraculous stuff, eh?" Flynn said. "I still don't comprehend how you did it, but I am glad you were able."

"Flynn?" Iviana spoke suddenly.

"Yes?"

"What do you *do*?"

Flynn looked up to the dark, twinkling sky, hands on his hips. "Odd jobs: hunting, mending, repairing; anything really. Anything that will keep me busy and provide for Laurel's needs."

"Do you like it?" she asked him.

He laughed. "Not exactly, but it's not the worst life a person could have; and I'm glad we've got Laurel's garden for steady income. She's a real talent with the greens, I can tell you that." He turned to her. "Why? What do *you* do? Go about performing miracles?"

She wavered. "I don't know yet. That's why I asked you. I was hoping to get an idea of what people do."

Flynn was confused. "What have you done up to now?"

Iviana shrugged. "I helped my mentor with her healing, gardening, oh, everything."

"But you wanted to get out and see the world?" he guessed.

"No. I just needed to leave... I couldn't be there. I don't have a home anymore."

"Did something... happen?" Flynn asked carefully.

Iviana nodded, but did not elaborate.

"Life is a... clumsy thing," Flynn commented. "I often wonder why I should be here at all."

"Here, as in *here*, with your sister?"

"No, no. This is the best place I know to be, though I know she'll marry eventually and I'll be forced to give her up. No, I mean *here*, on this planet, in this life. What's it for? I'm not doing it any good. I'm not really doing anything."

"Of course you are," Iviana disagreed. "You're the sort of man who lets dragons live, helps those in trouble, cares so wholly for his sister. The world needs more like you. Indeed, I have not known more than one person like you. I suppose you are a rarity, Flynn."

He smiled. "Perhaps I'll go about saving dragons for a living. Do they pay well?"

"Not really."

"Blast. Well, maybe when I've married off that sister of mine, I'll go out and see the world myself." Flynn took Iviana's hand and ran with her up to the house as he spoke, "Go wherever the wind takes me!"

Iviana chuckled. "That's a grand idea! Maybe you'll get your own dragon companion and he can fly you over the globe: the daring duo. That's what they'll call you."

"Ha! That's what they'll say of you someday, dragon-savior." He bowed as he said this and opened the door.

She rolled her eyes and shook her head. "I'll probably disappear into some cave, a hermit for eternity."

"Mm." He rubbed his chin and laughed. "Probably."

"Oh, thank you, *friend.*"

❧

The next few days consisted of hunting, gardening and attempts at flying. When the next afternoon Flynn came into the house with a pack full of hunted critters, Iviana demanded he show her how he achieved so much game.

"Haven't you a handy dragon for that?" he asked. "I would think he'd fetch you a feast every meal."

"He doesn't eat meat."

Flynn laughed. "You're joking?"

"No. I often wonder if he's offended when I enjoy it myself."

"Alright, then, Ivi." He patted her on the back. "Tomorrow I'll show you how it's done."

When Flynn called out, "Darlin' come!" Iviana realized the hunting trip would be far different than she had expected. At his call, a lovely brown falcon came flying in and landed on Flynn's fist. He introduced the ladies and proceeded in explaining the art of falconry.

"You thought I managed all that game alone," he teased Iviana.

She ignored him and concentrated on what she was being taught. It seemed it was she and Flynn's job to fish out critters so the falcon could hunt and kill them; then she and Flynn were left with the chore of finding the hunted prey. Though at first Iviana refused to believe the bird could offer much help, she eventually consented to the fact that it was more than helpful to have her along.

After they'd attained a great deal of game with Darlin', Flynn sent the falcon away with a token of food and fetched a bow and arrows. After several attempts at this form of hunt, Iviana wanted to give up, claiming she didn't have anything but a sword and would never need to know how to use a bow, but Flynn insisted, saying, "You never know when you'll be in dire need of the knowledge. Life is full of surprises."

After she begged they give it up for the day, Flynn moved on to the cudgel, insisting it would be far easier for a lady than the bow and arrow, anyway. Iviana glared at him and picked the bow up again.

"I'll master it before I leave," she promised.

Flynn chuckled hardily.

After her lessons in the days that followed, Flynn tried desperately to coax the dragon into liking him. It seemed the creature did not mind flying him about when Iviana accompanied, but when she was not there, the dragon would simply scoot away. Once, when Flynn tried offering him a plant he enjoyed as a treat, the dragon blew smoke into his face. After that, he tried apologizing for having tried to kill him, talking to him, petting, more treats, but the dragon would have none of it.

Finally, Flynn managed to get atop the dragon and encouraged him to take to the air. When the man landed with a nasty thud after the dragon somersaulted mid-air, he gave up.

"I can't blame it, really. I did bestow that scar." He pointed to the place where his sword had struck weeks ago.

"I think it's your personality, Flynn."

The man laughed. "I thank you, my lady."

"I wasn't kidding," she added laughingly. "You're not his type."

"It has a type?"

"You've got to stop calling him 'it.' That would be a start."

In the early evenings, Iviana taught Laurel about different plants and herbs with healing properties. She enjoyed being the one to share the knowledge for a change, but warned the girl that revealing she had such knowledge would be a mistake.

"I don't believe it," Laurel said. "You would think everyone would want to be friends with a healer."

"The problem is I've never met anyone with such knowledge, other than my mentor, of course. I've been called a witch the whole of my life because of my abilities. It's too incomprehensible for people."

"I wouldn't even mind if you were," Laurel admitted. "I think you're marvelous. What was it you did just as I was falling asleep that first night: the heat in my forehead?"

"What do you mean?" Iviana asked her, staring with open confusion.

"You touched my head after giving me the medicine. It was as if you released something into me and I felt so peaceful. You did it again later that night, I think. The memory's so cloudy now."

Iviana only stared at her intently and said, "I think you dreamed it, Laurel. I did no such thing."

೮౦

On her final evening, Iviana informed the household of her decision to leave the next morning.

"There is a supposed door in a cave and I'm longing to know what my dragon would show me there. He's become more anxious to go than I've seen him yet. It's time."

"We're sorry to see you go," Laurel answered her properly, then jumped up and hugged her friend. "Oh, I do wish you could stay. You will visit?"

"I think so," Iviana answered, "if it's alright with Flynn."

"Ay," Flynn said sadly. "If you bring me a souvenir." He winked. "Stay safe, dragon-savior. And make sure that dragon minds. He's an ornery beasty."

"Only to you," she responded.

The next morning Iviana woke early. Her dragon met her at the edge of the woods as though he knew she was coming and they flew into the sky before Flynn could hurry to meet them and say his last goodbye.

"Alright, my dragon, I'm in your hands now," she told him.

∞ 7 ∞

SOME DAYS LATER, the dragon at last found the place he wished to reveal. Lowering Iviana before a large, ominous mountain, the mystery of Jaela's Cavern leaped within her mind at the sight of it. Her very dear Naphtali had spoken of this place in her diary, but never to Iviana herself, an enigma that peeked her curiosity more than anything. She had always assumed, naively, that they had no secrets from one another. It had certainly been so on Iviana's part, but as she remembered her friend, she realized that, as she had been a very old woman, there must have been a great deal that Naphtali had never even mentioned. Even upon her death, she had only just begun to speak about Iviana's own birth-parents. What was this place that her mentor had been drawn to for help when she was so ill? And where was the door?

Having landed, Iviana procured the much-used diary and turned to the page concerning the door, reading it again.

"I regret to inform these tattered pages that I am ill and cannot find a cure in this realm. I have tried the door in Jaela's Cavern..."

Of course, the door must be inside the cavern that was in view at the foot of the mountain. Iviana peered upward, squinting her eyes against the sun, and took in the fullness of the peak. Immediately, she felt as though it was reading, even weighing the small, young woman before it.

Standing further back, it appeared a little like the ancient face of an old man, the cavern at the foot a terribly displaced mouth of the mountain man. Adding a sort of bearded, rustic appearance, green moss and grass glistened upon the great rock face. Its effect was strangely beautiful under the golden rays of the late afternoon sun.

Iviana, stepping up to the base of the mountain, discovered the rock was hot to the touch and sent tingles through her arm that felt almost like what she thought lightning might feel like, as if the mountain really was alive with some powerful charge. Even so, this could not be. It was all a great story she had conjured in her mind.

Still, it was difficult to venture into the cavern, especially when she was met with such an eery, uninviting sight. It was much larger on the inside than it had appeared from the outside for, though the entrance to the cave was small, its walls grew drastically once within.

Thick gray cobwebs draped from the ceiling and walls, whispering of untold secrets that wound their way through a tunnel at the far end of the cavern, almost as if pointing the way Iviana ought to go. The webs were sticky to the touch and attached themselves generously to her clothes and hair, causing her to shriek when first she entered.

Peering beyond the webs, there were dozens of yellowed ivory candles covered in dust, webbing and their own melted wax that appeared as though they floated off the walls on old iron sconces. It seemed as if, at one time, they'd been used often by some person past.

Iviana pulled the flint from her pack and struck it against her sword to light one. Stealing the candle from its sconce, she lifted it to better view her surroundings and revealed large, grotesque spiders cloaking the entire cavern. Though the repellent creatures crawled over her booted feet, they seemed content to ignore the mountain's trespasser for the time being. Goosebumps crept down Iviana's arms, but she stood her ground. Even so, the uneasy intruder cast a pensive glance to where her dragon remained outside. She could trust him, couldn't she?

A few steps more and Iviana was certain she was being observed—not by the spiders, but by the unseen eyes of every wall, nook and crevice, as if they were reporting what they saw to the grandfather mountain. She could not help but look for some figure hiding in a corner, spying on her every move. Though she found no such thing, she did find a portion of the wall that was lacking candles.

Here, there were very old etchings, almost illegible. Upon closer examination, the forms of dragons began to take shape. Numerous dragons— more than she would ever have guessed existed at one time—surrounded what looked like an extremely large, even oversized, fire-pit. The dragons gazed into the flames with their mesmerizing eyes, but their eyes were not like those of her dragon; they were filled with the reflection of the flames. She wondered why the artist had taken time to add this detail, as the rest of the picture appeared rough and hurried.

It was interesting, to say the least, but it did not have much to do with the questions racing through her mind. She simply could not shake the feeling that this place was marked by something—by some unseen force or ancient act so powerful it had left traces of the occurrence. There were no physical signs to indicate anything of the kind, however, aside from the etching on the wall.

Who was this Jaela, anyway, that this cavern was named for? Iviana began to wonder. *What had she been or done that this place should be named for her?*

At the mere acknowledgment of the name in her mind, the whole mountain quaked, mildly, and a shiver ran up and down her body. She moved on then, allowing the candlelight to lead her through the passage at the far end: the tunnel where the spiderwebs led.

To Iviana's shock and dismay, the spiders in the cavern gathered around and followed her into the tunnel. Her better judgment would have guided her straight out of the mountain, never to return to such a place, but her heart was guiding her and she wished to discover what Naphtali had not told her.

As she continued through the tunnel, crouching over and around fallen rocks, following the constant winding of the tiny passage, the spiders never harmed Iviana and rarely did they set foot on her. For this she was grateful, for the winding of the tunnel nearly pushed her agility to its limits, the way she was forced to move at times, and she had no thought to spare for the followers.

After what seemed like hours, Iviana grew so weary she paused and looked back at the way she had come. Setting her candle on the ground, she was deciding whether she should return to her dragon when her foot edged backward and she stumbled abruptly into nothingness. The young woman screamed and frantically flailed her arms about for something to grab onto as the pit grew deeply black.

This is it, Iviana thought.

Her mind calmly wrapped around her fate when suddenly her pack caught on something and she was harshly jerked to a halt. She reached her arm back to where she was held fast and felt a cold, dangling, metal chain. She gasped and thanked the chain for saving her, as if it were a token from the mountain.

She realized now that, had she been paying better attention, the chain would have swung her across the chasm that had unfortunately escaped her notice. *Oh, well,* she thought, *now is not the time to scold oneself.* What she needed was to focus on how to get out of her current predicament. She was alive—and she was grateful—but how she was going to loosen her pack from the chain in order to climb it without falling to her death was beyond her.

Now she was caught in the abyss, she determined, almost as an offering to her possible demise, to continue through the tunnel to its end... if she survived. The tunnel could not be only a natural crevice in the mountain, for someone must have attached the chain she was now dangling from. Oh, this wonderful, lifesaving chain and pack: they had worked together to rescue her.

Her pack. She needed to free one arm from it and swing herself around so the front of her body was facing the chain and she could grasp it with both hands.

Slowly, she forced her arm from the tight grip of the pack's strap wrapped over her shoulder; but this was not as simple as she had hoped, for there came a point where her arm did not wish to budge. The weight of her body was forcing the straps to hold her mercilessly. She tried for some time to release her arm from the strap, but with each attempt, it was clutching her more closely. Her arm was forming a faint rope burn now and the lack of circulation felt like hundreds of tiny pinpricks on her arms.

"GAAAH!" she roared into the abyss around her, giving into fear and frustration. She was breathing hard from the fight to free her arm and was soon blinking back the first onset of tears.

You'll die here, utterly alone, a wicked voice whispered from the abyss.

No, no, another voice interrupted, *you'll go mad before it comes to that. You know you can't bear being alone.*

"Stop it!" Iviana pleaded. Her head limp, she gave a sob. The voices ceased, but her own thoughts did the work of any number of taunts. From the darkness, the voices had spoken truth and she knew it. She had left her home because she couldn't tolerate loneliness. She was fragile and did not possess the strength to handle life on her own. Perhaps she had been too sheltered and relied on her mentor too much. If only Naphtali had lived long enough to help her stand on her own two feet; a little warning would have been helpful...

All alone... all alone, her mind taunted. She sobbed again.

Sweet Ivi, you are never alone, a nearly audible voice whispered into her heart.

Iviana raised her head, filled with unbidden tenacity. She could not remain dangling forever, left to die and rot on this chain. With a sudden, heart–stopping yank, she freed her arm and instantly reached to grip the chain. The spontaneous act was a success, her pack now dangling from her elbow. She had decided she was willing to lose it if she absolutely had to, but with Naphtali's diary within, she was glad it had not come to it.

The climb up the chain was not something Iviana wished to repeat, but she finally reached the passage where her candle lay, still lit. After bringing herself into a swinging motion, she leaped back to the ledge where she'd left it and wrapped the heavy chain around a jagged piece of rock.

Oh, how this rocky, rugged ground soothed her nerves as she sprawled over it. The uncomfortable bit of earth would never have tempted her before the climb, but now it was as good as a fluffy featherbed.

❦ 8 ❧

IVIANA AWOKE WITH a start. Not having meant
to sleep, she hoped there would be enough candle to
continue her journey. Turning to examine it, it was
apparent a good amount of time had passed while
she'd been sleeping there.

What stunned her first were the spiders
blanketing her body, though upon further
investigation and much squealing and leaping, they
had not harmed her. What further astonished her was
that neither chain nor chasm was anywhere to be
found. Iviana gasped and huffed over this and would
have dismissed it as a dream after a forgotten blow to
the head, but her muscles were sore from the climb
and the rope burn on her shoulder remained.
Nevertheless, Iviana felt she had no choice but to
continue her trek through the tunnel.

Iviana knew she was nearing her destination

when the spiders ceased following her, as if they knew something unusual loomed further on. The hairs on her arms stood on end as she rounded the next corner and the heart of the mountain was before her.

Here, there was nothing but a large, brilliant red door. When she stepped up to it, however, it stunned her, for it was not very large at all, but of rather average size. It was, indeed, quite common aside from its brilliant crimson hue and the fact that it was evidently quite old. Upon further inspection, the door's knob was unlike anything she had seen before. It was a rich, glowing gold and should have been caked in dust as the rest of the door was, but had somehow escaped it. Instead, it shined—almost sparkled—and held the face of a beautiful, ancient-looking dragon.

Iviana wondered if it was safe to touch it, to tamper with this aged door, or if she should let it be and return to what little normalcy her life still held. But did she really desire normalcy? Her mentor had not been what was considered "normal" and yet she loved Naphtali more than anything. Her dragon's friendship, too, was uncommon as well, but she was thankful she had been blessed with the meeting. And all the average townsfolk who had rejected and ignored the women who continually healed their wounded, sick and dying, they, in return, had been less than grateful. They responded by making up stories about Naphtali.

She remembered a time when she'd been collecting berries from a patch of bushes near the town and had overheard the conversation of a group of girls a little older than she.

"My mother would whip me if she knew I was spoiling my dinner with these berries," one girl said.

"Mm, mine too, but we never have berries at my house. My mother thinks they're cursed," an orange-haired girl spoke.

Another girl giggled. "Why does she think that?"

"Well..." the carrot-top gave the group a devious expression and motioned for them to lean in close. Why she felt the need to do so was beyond Iviana for the girls were unaware that anyone else was near. "Just before I was born, my grandmother got really sick, so my daddy went to see the witch lady."

Iviana grimaced at the name, knowing to whom she was referring and wounded by the thought that these people had actually given her mentor the nickname "witch lady."

"She gave him an ugly looking liquid made up of mulberries and whatever else witches use to bring

about their miracles. Anyway, he trusted the old lady and gave the stuff to my grandmother and I guess she died a few minutes later. My mother cried, saying the old witch had poisoned her and my daddy got really mad. He gathered up a few men from the town to confront the hag, but she denied the whole thing, saying grandmother must have been too close to death for her work to have taken any affect on her."

Iviana's stomach grew sick from the girl's story. She hated the way the girl was talking about her dear Naphtali and was filled with indignation for her friend, knowing it must have been difficult for her to endure. She longed to run away, but was afraid the girls would see her.

The girl telling the story continued, "She must have used her witchery to calm my daddy down because he believed her. When he told my mama about it she was furious that he hadn't done away with the old lady. So, Mother went out, ready to give the old hag a piece of her mind, but before she got to the witch's house, she spotted her by these mulberry bushes, putting an angry curse on them and anyone who eats them!"

The girls in the group gasped and spat out their berries as the storyteller tossed another berry into her mouth, feigning bravery. Iviana thought it obvious the girl had made up the last part of the story, if not all of it. If, indeed, her mentor was a witch, why would she put a curse on the berries when she could just curse the angry family instead? This logic had not dawned on the little girls however, so they rose to leave, each vowing never to eat another berry again. They were some feet away when Iviana also rose, but as she did, she stumbled over a rock and fell through the mulberry bushes, letting out a small, short scream as she went. At the sound of her fall, the girls turned to see her fallen form and squealed cying the little witch-girl was coming after them to fulfill the curse and they ran with all their might toward home. As they ran, Iviana did as well. She ran crying all the way home and threw herself into the arms of her beloved friend.

"Naphtali, why do people make up stories about us?" she asked through sobs.

The older woman drew the girl into a chair and stroked her hair. "Because they fear what they do not know; what they refuse to know."

"Why don't they get to know us?"

"They don't understand what it is I—we—do and that also scares them."

"They're cowards," Iviana whispered in anger.

"No, they're fairly ordinary as far as people go, I'm afraid."

"I don't want to be ordinary then," Iviana declared.

The older woman gave a half-smile at that. "Good. Don't be. Be my courageous girl."

She didn't feel very courageous now—frightened of a door—but the knob was like the eyes of her dragon, mesmerizing in its rugged surroundings and she just... she had to turn it or at least touch it and feel the exquisite thing in her palm. She looked around, as though afraid someone was watching and would try to stop her, then back at the door. She studied the cracks around the door frame, wanting to glimpse what was on the other side, but they were too dirt-filled. She looked at the knob again and decided it may be easier not to try it, for it filled her with an excitement she did not understand and this intimidated her. Yes, she faced the thought again, she was afraid of a door.

"Just turn it!" Iviana yelled aloud. As she did, her hand jumped, almost involuntarily, and touched the knob. But before she could turn it, a bright light filled her vision, white and blinding. She tried to shut her eyes against it, but the light was so blaring it blinded her even as she closed her eyes.

A voice spoke and the light grew more tolerable.

"If you have been allowed to enter this domain, then you are of the Greater Archipelagos," said a booming, matter-of-fact voice. "Listen well."

Stunned by what was happening, Iviana fell to a sitting position on the ground like a child who's just taken its first steps, but doesn't quite have the balance for it. Still, her vision was filled with light. She could not even make out dim outlines of what lay around her, but she was absently glad that at least the light did not burn as it had at first.

As the voice continued, a foggy vision began to form before her eyes. It was cloudy, as though she was flying and looking down on a land beneath the clouds. She could just make out dozens of small green islands and assumed this to be the "Greater Archipelagos" of which the voice had spoken.

The voice continued, "Though you know it or not, our great blood flows through your veins. A dragon has recognized this and has shown you the cave-mouth in hopes of returning you to us. However, it is apparent you are a stranger to our lands, and will not be able to enter, or the knob would have turned within the first moment you grasped it. Fear not, oh, kinsman. Should destiny permit, you will find your way to us."

With that, Iviana's eyesight became normal again and the voice ceased. She blinked and looked around, amazed to find herself once again in the cave. She grabbed at the doorknob and tried to turn it again and again, but it would not budge nor did the voice and light return. At this, anger began to well in her. She was exhausted from the journey through the cave and now it was to no avail. Why could they not have placed the door a little closer to the mouth of the cave so that their "kinsman" or whoever would not have to journey so far only to be rejected by a doorknob?

"Hellooo!" she called and banged on the door with both fists. "Let me in!" She was pounding with every bit of strength she had left. "Please, let me in! Is this how you treat your 'kin'?"

She did not understand her desperate need to get to the other side of the door and this frustrated her further, so she pounded repeatedly until, slowly, she fell to the ground in exhaustion, but was no less frustrated. There, alone in the cave, she began to sob, first quietly, then loudly.

If what the voice had said was true, that the blood of those that lived on those islands ran within her, then there was a place she belonged where perhaps she would finally be accepted. Instead, she was left in this cold, musty cave, all alone, once again. She continued crying beside the door until her candle ceased to burn and she drifted into unconsciousness once again.

છ

After nearly two days wait, the dragon could not sense Iviana had gone through the door, so he grew worried. As his form was too large to enter, he took to the sky. It was yet another day before he returned with Flynn. Though Flynn did not know why he was needed, he could sense the urgency of the dragon and hoped it would not be too late.

Flynn made his way into the cave and stole a candle from one of the sconces. He spared no time to look around, for his focus was on finding Iviana. Realizing he had nothing to light it with, he carried the candle outside and shifted his weight from one leg to the other, still a little nervous of the dragon.

"Uuh, I could use a light... buddy?"

The dragon did not move, but a fire appeared on the wick. Flynn was confused, but thanked the dragon and entered the cave again. He made his way through the tunnel, as Iviana had, but when he reached the place where the chasm had been, there was still no chasm at all. Instead, he found a tiny piece of wax where the stump of Iviana's candle had been and hoped he was close.

It was hours, however, before the hairs on his arms stood on end and goosebumps fanned over him. The tunnel veered to the left and it was there he found Iviana and got his first clear look at the door. The nearness of it sent another wave of goosebumps and, though his curiosity was great, he focused his attention on Iviana.

Placing the back of his hand to her forehead and cheeks, he found that she was burning with fever. He tried to wake her, but her eyelids did not even twitch.

"Alright, dearie," he muttered as he hefted her over his shoulder. "Lets get you out of here."

He cast another longing glance at the door before returning to the dragon.

Iviana did not wake that night. Flynn did everything he could for her, but his knowledge of such things was menial. By morning, he looked to the dragon as though communicating there was nothing he could do.

The dragon stood and waited.

Flynn wasn't certain how, but he knew what the dragon wanted and lifted Iviana onto his back.

"Take care of her," he said.

The dragon responded by letting a tiny whiff of smoke curl out of his nostrils. Flynn took the hint and stepped back as he watched the two fly into the sky.

As soon as they were out of sight, Flynn made his way into the mouth of the cave. All that night he'd felt the door calling him and was determined to investigate.

ॐ

The dragon flew for days without rest, while Iviana slept fitfully on his back. Not once was she near falling, for the dragon flew carefully. When the landmark that told him they were in the right place was in view, he knew he must wake her or what needed to happen next would not be possible. The dragon landed and slowly dropped her there, then paced around her, uncertain of what to do next. He tried nudging her arms and legs with his muzzle, but she did not wake. He rolled her over and over on the ground and still she showed no signs of consciousness. He could not smell death on her, but knew it would sink its claws into her if he could not get her to help.

Finally, he put his face before hers and gently blew his hot, hot breath into it. It burned her eyes and her pale face turned red, but slowly she awoke. At first she did not dare open her eyes, for the heat was too intense. She was barely conscious and did not know where she was or what was happening, only flailed her hands before her face as though trying to stop the inexplicable heat. It took a little time for her to cool, but slowly raised her eyelids when she felt it was safe.

"Dragon," she whispered. She was weak and her throat was dry.

The dragon nudged her head with his nose, trying to wake her more fully, but to no avail.

"Water," she whispered hoarsely.

The dragon knew what she needed, but could not help her, for they were currently in a dry, rocky wasteland. If Iviana could only awaken enough to hold onto him while he flew her into the other world, there would be plenty of everything she needed there.

She began to lose consciousness again and the dragon pushed her over onto her stomach. Her mouth fell open over the dusty surface, filling it with the taste of dry dirt. This upset her, so she found enough strength to push herself up with her hands and into a kneeling position. She was too weak to speak, but she glared at the beast.

He turned, waiting for her to crawl onto his back.

Iviana took a long, shaky breath, trying to muster the strength to do what the dragon wished. She attempted to stand, but her legs could not support the full weight of her body, so she collapsed to the ground where she determined to remain. Even so, the dragon kicked dirt into her face until she was up again.

She crawled over to the dragon, who immediately crouched down to make it easier for her to pull herself onto him. Had she been more alert, she would have found it remarkable just how flat he managed to make himself.

Once on his back, the dragon took to the air, but Iivana was not hanging on as she needed to, so the dragon slowly arched upwards, allowing the girl to slide down his back and, out of instinct, she latched onto him with her arms and legs. He sighed a little in relief at finally having gotten what he wanted and began his flight upward.

The dragon flew higher and faster with every breath he took and soon they were rocketing into the stars. Beyond the clouds and the blue sky they went until they were surrounded by a dark, sparkling sky and, though the girl somehow managed to hold on tightly, she was not conscious enough to fully experience the trip.

However, there was a bright, blinding light that stunned her to full consciousness as they entered a sort of shining vortex. They were moving so quickly Iviana could not catch her breath. She was near fainting before they reached the end and were lightly tossed out into a calm blue sky with clouds drifting silently around them. It made her feel as though what had just happened, had been a dream and she allowed herself to rest once again.

∞ 9 ∞

THE WITCH OF whom Flynn had found it difficult to admit his fraternizing with to Iviana watched in irritation as the ancient dragon flew away with Iviana. It was this witch, who went by the name of Aradia, that had told Flynn she would help his ill sister if he would bring her the heart of a dragon.

She had watched through her enchanted looking glass when Flynn had actually succeeded in finding one and had nearly slayed it... but that *girl* had stopped him. What were the chances that some mysterious, dragon-loving female with big blue eyes would come along just as he had been ready to cut the dragon's heart from its chest?

After watching his failure in irritation, she had sent a random band of men to do her bidding. She'd sent them to bring Flynn to her, that she might "persuade" the boy to find the dragon again, but they, too, had failed. They had not been desperate enough; they had not cared enough. She knew better than to count on those who were not desperate for one reason or another. The passionate glimmer in Flynn's eyes as he had begged her to help his sister proved that he could find what she asked of him... if given enough reason.

She had consulted her dark craft as to where she might find him herself and had been shown Jaela's Cavern. The very place spurred her hatred and made even more important her mission. She would further her revenge on the world beyond that door in the cave, the very door that would not allow her to pass through, though it was her birthright. So it became all the more essential she get hold of a dragon's heart. That was to be her key to pass through worlds.

However, as she arrived on the scene and found Flynn sending that irritating young woman off with the dragon again, she began to think up a new plan altogether. The mysterious girl might be more useful to her than even a dragon and she could still use Flynn to fetch what she needed.

∞10∞

IVIANA AWOKE TO find herself in a soft bed, covered with pure white linens. The canopy that stretched over the entire ceiling was of pure white and the walls that enclosed the room were a rich ivory. There were white, semi-transparent curtains over the large opening in the wall she faced that opened into a large, private patio. She was determined to have a look outside when a woman entered through the sheer white curtains over the doorway to her right.

"Oh, you're awake!" the woman said. "Good. I was just going to wake you. I'm sure your stomach is desperate for nourishment." She laid a tray on Iviana's lap that consisted of a large bowl of rather thin looking soup and a grainy roll.

Iviana responded eagerly looking the tray over, "Thank you. This looks delicious."

The woman gave a small, pleasant smile. "I know it's very little, but we thought we'd start you off with something light. You've been unconscious for some time."

Iviana nodded and took a spoonful of the soup. Swallowing, she inquired, "We?"

"Yes. Your presence here has been the subject on every tongue and everyone has an opinion on what should be done with you." The lady ended with a wink. Iviana nodded and dunked a hunk of bread into the broth.

The woman hesitated at the doorway for an instant, looking as though she was motioning to someone outside of the door with her eyes. She turned to Iviana.

"I'll let you finish your meal. Someone will be in to check on you in a little while."

After finishing the meal, Iviana decided to try standing. Her legs were weak and stiff as she made her way over to the patio's door frame and peeked through the white chiffon curtain. Beyond the patio was a long spread of creamy white beach outlining an ocean of the bluest water she had ever seen. The sun was beaming down with all its might as she stepped outside onto the marble-floored patio. Iviana closed her eyes and smiled. She felt an overwhelming peace in this moment and could not bring herself to care that she had no idea where she was neither was she altogether worried about how she had arrived. Opening her eyes again, her nonchalance was reaffirmed, for the view was breathtaking.

Iviana knew she should not venture out into this strange place in nothing but a nightgown and no one to invite her, but the shoreline was undeniably calling her. She swiftly made her way across the beach. Just before reaching the water's edge, she stopped and looked down at what was beneath her feet. The softness of the sand was like nothing she'd felt before. Curious, she bent down to take some into her hand. It was while examining its texture that she looked up for a moment and caught a glimpse of the clear water only a few feet ahead of her. She was drawn to it and quickly dropped the sand to move closer.

Its clarity was impossible. For a moment she wondered if it was not water at all, but some other unknown liquid. She knelt and dipped her hands in to taste it. It was water, after all, but the sweetest, purest water she had ever tasted. It befuddled her, for she had always heard ocean water was salty, but this water did not fit that description at all. Its flavor offered a hint of honey and it cooled her throat as it went down, providing a most pleasant experience.

She stood immediately. What was this place?

"I see you've gained your strength back quickly," a young woman's voice spoke from behind her.

Iviana turned, caught off guard."I-I'm sorry. I-"

The young woman with long blonde hair giggled. "Oh, I wasn't accusing. My mother wouldn't let me meet you earlier; she said you needed rest, but I see you're not as weak as she thought."

Iviana nodded and looked around her. "This is beautiful, but... where am I?"

"My mother didn't tell you?" the blonde woman asked, obviously surprised. "Your daring dragon has brought you into the Greater Archipelagos," she raised an eyebrow conspiratorially, "without permission."

Iviana let that sink in a moment. "Without permission? What does that mean?"

"Well, it's silly, if you ask me, but we are a very solitary community. We rather like to keep to ourselves in our little world, you see." She waited a moment before continuing, "Very, very much to ourselves. As in, even if you're a relative of ours, if you weren't born in our realm, you probably never would have been given permission to enter."

Iviana didn't know how to respond. A thousand

and one questions raced through her mind and she couldn't seem to slow them. Her head grew woozy and everything was going dark. Next thing Iviana knew, she was back in her white bed with the woman who had brought her the food—and was apparently the blond girl's mother—hovering over her.

"My dear, how are you feeling?" the woman asked. "You shouldn't have gone out on your first day of consciousness. It really isn't a wonder you fainted." When Iviana didn't respond, she went on. "I think you should know you were not in great shape when Tragor brought you to us. It was all we could do to keep you alive; our Healer wore himself to a frazzle." The woman's eyes softened and she finished with, "Now, I only tell you this so you know the gravity of your condition and allow yourself rest."

Guilt immediately swept over Iviana. "I didn't mean to be any trouble-"

"Oh, no, my dear girl," the woman interrupted, "please understand me. I am immensely grateful that you're here." She gazed out the open curtains to the beach. "More grateful than you know." She turned back to Iviana and smiled. "Just be comfortable. Is there anything I can do for you?"

"Yes," Iviana answered immediately. "I have... so

many questions." The primary being who this Tragor was.

"I'm sure you do," the blonde girl's mother answered compassionately, "but now is not the time. Now, here's some tea, drink up!—and sleep."

Iviana did drink the tea, but she couldn't sleep. She wondered how she could be related to these people. They were so different from her—so graceful and lovely. They were so foreign. She had no memory of her mother, and Naphtali never spoken of her father. For whatever reason, she'd never wondered much about them. Knowing that her parents had left her with Naphtali and taken off was enough for her. She had no interest in people who had abandoned her. Instead, she had clung to Naphtali, who had been her mentor, mother and friend and was all she needed. But she was gone now.

Iviana rested in her room over the course of that day as well as the next, until around noon of her third day. During that time, she had no visitors aside from the same woman who came to check on her and bring her food, whose name she eventually learned was Naii. Naii had taken Iviana's time of rest very seriously and didn't allow anyone to disturb her. This made for an incredibly boring few days, so

Iviana was very grateful when Naii's daughter brought her lunch on that third day.

"Please, tell me I'm off bed-duty," Iviana pleaded.

The young blonde girl giggled easily, "Yes, and, if you are feeling up to it, you are to attend a banquet tonight as guest of honor," she admitted with glee. "It'll have a spectacular surprise. I arranged it myself," she ended proudly.

This was not exactly the sort of news Iviana was hoping for. First of all, she'd never been to a banquet. Secondly, she was only somewhat acquainted with this young woman and her mother and she wasn't certain she felt ready to be around so many strangers at once. Then again, no one, aside from Naphtali, had ever wished to celebrate her before—at least not before she had healed Flynn's sister. That, combined with the satisfaction on the blonde girl's face, encouraged Iviana to hold her tongue on the matter. Instead, she answered with, "May I ask your name?"

"I haven't introduced myself?" the young woman answered, exasperated. "I'm Nimua. All the women in my family have 'N' names. I think it's strange, too, but it's a family tradition." She paused before, "And, don't tell me: you're Iviana."

Iviana wasn't surprised at her knowing her

name. She assumed she'd heard it from Naii. "Ivi, yes," she replied.

"So, he was right... extraordinary." The girl's attention drifted to some unknown place.

"Nimua?" Iviana called her back. "Who was right?"

"Marquen. He's... a little eccentric. Alright, he can be very eccentric. I'm pretty much the only person who talks to him. He told me you'd be coming soon and a few days later, well, here you are."

"But... how could he have known I was coming? *I* didn't even know..."

"I don't know. I've just learned to trust what he says. He's always right. Now, you'd better eat up. My mother will be in soon and I'm needed to help prepare for the banquet. I'll see you later."

ॐ

Just as Nimua promised, her mother arrived shortly after her departure.

"What have you been doing with these hands?" Naii asked as she worked on manicuring them.

"I–I don't know. I didn't know it wasn't good to

use your hands."

Naii smiled. "Well, you can use them; just don't beat them. I suppose it's from the use of that sword." She gestured to the weapon sitting on a wooden table across the room.

Iviana nodded.

"How did you come upon it?" Naii asked her. "It looks quite peculiar."

"Naphtali, my guardian, gave it to me."

"Naphtali?" Naii stopped her work.

Iviana sat up straight and answered, "Yes. Why?"

"She was born here... and grew up here. If it's the same Naphtali." She studied Iviana. "Yes, I think it must be. Naphtali is not your mother."

"No, she isn't—wasn't," Iviana corrected herself.

Naii hesitated. "She is no longer living?"

Iviana cast her eyes upon the floor. "No."

"I see," Naii answered. Iviana was surprised to see Naii's eyes fill with tears. "I'm sorry," she muttered and tried to stop the tears from falling with her baggy sleeve. "How did you come to know her? Was she... was she friends with your mother?"

"I don't know, exactly. I lived with Naphtali for as long as I can remember and I don't remember my mother at all."

"Hmm." Naii grew thoughtful and the two fell

silent. When she'd finished doing what she could with Iviana's hands, she stood and gathered her things. "Now, you must bathe."

Iviana, felt her hair and skin. "No kidding."

Naii couldn't help grinning and stifled a laugh. "I'll have your bath prepared. Someone will fetch you when it's ready."

She made ready to leave, but there was one thing Iviana had to ask before she did.

"Do you know who my mother was?"

Naii hesitated and wouldn't look Iviana in the eyes. "I believe so." She paused before ending with, "I'll be back to escort you to the banquet" and left the room.

A little while later, a small group of very graceful women came to fetch Iviana and escort her to a wash room where they bathed and scrubbed the girl in perfumed water until her skin stung. She wondered that they cared to leave any skin on her body at all, but when they'd finished, they applied lotions that helped to ease the pain until she felt light and clean and her skin glowed.

After this, the women sat Iviana down and manipulated her dark curls so they hung loosely from her head and off her neck. They fastened tiny gold beads that twinkled like glowing stars on her head in a band just where little curls dangled over her face.

Then the women stood her on her feet and dressed her in a long, flowing, white tunic lined with gold at the hem. Over the tunic they placed a white, loose-fitting top with sleeves made up of the material from the bodice that was drawn up and tied at her shoulders. They secured this around her waste with a brown belt that looked as though it was made of vines. As they wrapped a long, white drape over her arms, she glanced in the mirror and felt as though she was staring at a stranger.

"You really like white here," she mumbled

Naii entered the room as the women chuckled and commented, "Don't be afraid of beauty, Iviana. I don't think you can avoid it, anyway."

Naii linked her arm through Iviana's and led her out the front of the building where she had been staying. When she looked back at it, Iviana realized it was quite small and not much bigger than the cottage she'd grown up in.

Naii noticed what she was looking at and said, "This is your personal quarters for now. It is normally reserved for guests—those who may have returned from travel or those from other islands who have need to stay with us for a time. We do not have many visitors from the outside—or any, really. You are a special case, which makes you something of great interest to everyone." Naii noticed Iviana's nerves heighten and added, "I suppose I should warn you now: they will stare. They will not mean to be rude, but of course that does not mean they will refrain from it. We don't receive visitors from outside our realm so we are not used to requiring manners suitable for such guests."

As Naii led her along a narrow path, there were little homes everywhere. Most were much like her guest house. They were all small square buildings with white columns on either side of the door covered in little intricate moldings of grape vines or ivy around the top and base of the columns. Some had green, flowery vines creeping over the whole of the building with flower boxes under some of the windows. These buildings were scattered here and there, with no apparent rhyme or reason, but skinny paths managed to connect each one to the others.

Not all had the beautiful ocean view hers did. There were also tropical trees Iviana never knew existed and the grass that stretched over every inch of the island was the most brilliant, bright green she had ever beheld.

Bordering the path she and Naii were following—it appeared to be a main path though it was not very big and there were very few people actually using it—were rustic poles with lit torches to guide the way as afternoon gave way to evening. She could see in the distance many little lights twinkle to life as the islanders worked on illuminating the path ahead of them.

This place was a paradise, if ever Iviana had imagined one. The air was warm but crisp and perfumed by the scent of tropical flowers and honey. Above them, Iviana beheld a sky unlike any sky she had ever seen. She gasped aloud as she surveyed the twinkling diamonds, twice the number she was used to viewing in an evening sky. They lit the night beautifully, leaving little need for torches. There were smears of translucent pinks and purples relaying galaxies she had never viewed before. And then... she knew, she just *knew* this was not the same sky as the one she had looked upon so many times in Kierelia.

"It *is* stunning, isn't it?" Naii said dreamily as she peered upon the view, as if she'd forgotten it was there.

Finally, they reached the Grand Pavilion, the place where the feast was to be held. There were over a hundred noisy people standing, sitting, preparing and communing within a long, brightly lit, rectangular structure. It did not have walls or roof to enclose it. Rather, white marble columns that rose from the foundation formed a boundary. Limestone beams decorated with elaborately detailed etched grape vines connected the tops of the columns. Iviana was surprised to discover it had no roof and later learned the islanders refused to believe it would ever rain while they banqueted and, truth be told, it rarely ever did.

"Ivi!" Nimua called, rushing up to her.

"I'll leave you with my daughter now," Naii told Iviana as she shot a meaningful glare at a man who was staring at the island's guest. "I have some things to attend to." She gave the girl an encouraging squeeze on the shoulder. "Hold your head high. You'll be fine." Naii looked to Nimua who nodded in agreement.

Nimua took Iviana by the hand and excitedly led her into the grand hall overflowing with people. "Come on!" she said. "Darist is saving us seats, but I doubt he'll be able to hold them much longer." She led the way through the crowd of people, who did, indeed, stare as Iviana was led past them. She could feel the heat creeping up her neck and over her face. She wasn't at all used to so much attention or so many people together at once or even the level of noise.

Everyone was enjoying themselves as a merry, ethereal song flowed from a band of musical players in the middle of the room. There were silent, auspicious old women glaring as they lounged on their large pillows. Younger islanders chased each other while a small group of teenage girls heartily sang along with the music in a tongue Iviana couldn't understand. A young man stole a feather from a young woman's hair. The young woman squealed as she tried to snatch it back.

Finally, they reached a place where a tall, tan young man was guarding a couple of huge deep purple pillows with gold detail. Two young women about Iviana's age seemed to be attempting to snatch the pillows from him.

"Ah, here they are," the young man said and motioned for Nimua and Iviana to hurry over. The girls who'd been quarreling over the spot left disappointed as Nimua and Iviana seated themselves.

"I thought I would have to carry them off over my shoulders if they wouldn't leave," the young man said with a large grin.

Nimua rolled her eyes. "Thankfully we arrived before you were forced to show such a feat of strength."

"Oh, don't be such a shrew, Nimua," the man said heartily. "You have to admit you were impressed the day I carried the monument of Old Lady Alfri all the way across the island."

"Yes, and I was incredibly impressed when you dropped it just as you were placing it over the Ancestral Fountain, too," Nimua replied.

"Psh, no harm done," he replied easily.

"No harm? I don't recall Keneth's toe surviving the accident."

"Keneth was just fine after a few weeks and the statue stands proudly to this day. Now, stop being rude and introduce me to our guest."

Nimua forfeited. "Ivi, this is Darist. Darist, the lovely, mysterious Iviana."

"Iviana," the young man attempted an air of mock superiority, "allow me the honor of welcoming you on behalf of the entire Greater Archipelagos."

"I don't think that's your job, dimwit," Nimua cracked.

Darist smiled, despite the remark. "I welcome you on behalf of myself then. Tell me, how are you enjoying your stay? Are we treating you well?" he asked with a tiny gleam of humor in his eyes.

Iviana was grateful he didn't treat her with intrigued surprise like every other pair of eyes was.

"Very well, thank you. This island is... well, it's unlike anything I've seen." She answered as confidently as she could, but couldn't help feeling shy in the midst of the crowd of people.

"I'm sure it is, considering you're in another universe entirely," he remarked.

Iviana was shaken by the remark. Another universe? She recalled that Naii had mentioned something like it earlier, but the word hadn't sunk in at the time. "What do you mean?" she whispered hoarsely. Suddenly, her throat was too dry for words.

"Don't frighten her!" Nimua burst out. "Mother says they haven't explained things to her yet."

"No, please, "Iviana urged. "I'd really like 'things' explained to me now."

Darist answered her with regret, "I'm sure you would, but I don't think it's up to us to do it. I do wish we could."

Nimua squeezed her hand. "Don't worry. You trust your dragon, right? Well, he's the one who brought you here. He wouldn't have done so if he hadn't felt it was correct. You'll have your explanation soon, I'm sure."

Just then, select islanders began to walk around with large trays of food. There were fruits, vegetables and breads as well as dishes she'd never before enjoyed.

A girl came up to the three with a tray full of a fluffy fruit they called jujii. It was green the color of olives and smelled horrible, but with some prodding, Iviana consented to try it and discovered it was delicious.

After that, Iviana stuffed herself with whatever Nimua and Darist told her to and enjoyed nearly everything. Though, eventually, Iviana noticed a complete lack of meat.

"Do you not eat meat?" she asked them.

Nimua replied hesitantly, "I had heard you eat the beasts in your world. I wonder what it would taste like." Nimua cringed. "I really can't imagine it."

"I noticed my dragon doesn't either," Iviana commented.

"Yes, they had to give it up when they decided to make their home here years and years ago."

Iviana let out an exasperated sigh.

"What's the matter?" Darist asked.

"There are so many things I don't understand. I feel... overwhelmed."

"Take it one step at a time," Nimua encouraged. "I'll help you feel as comfortable as I can. You haven't even had a tour yet. I'll take care of that tomorrow."

Suddenly, a woman with long, flowing gray hair

stepped onto the platform where the musicians were assembled. Silence filled the assemblage. The woman was obviously older, but appeared ageless, somehow. As hard as Iviana tried, she could not determine the woman's age. Each time the woman moved, some feature on her face would confuse her.

"As you all know," the lady began in a deep, booming voice, "we have a guest among us. I would like to formally introduce her now and I will ask that the young lady please stand."

Iviana froze. This was the last thing she cared to do. In the silence, with all eyes focused on her, she began to feel dizzy. Nimua nudged her and the woman on the platform cleared her throat. Iviana's face turned a lovely shade of scarlet, but she could not move. She longed to run away into the dark.

Darist rose and offered Iviana his hand; it was all she could do to take it and allow him to lift her onto her feet. Once she was standing, he remained behind her for moral support and, looking around, she thought no one seemed to have noticed the occurrence except the ageless woman on the platform, who had an impatient expression on her face.

Her powerful voice continued, "Iviana... welcome to the Greater Archipelagos." At the older woman's words, the sound of applause roared across the perimeter as though she'd spoken a moving war-cry before going into battle. The lady quieted the assemblage with a wave of her hands and continued. "Iviana, we hereby acknowledge you as our kin, according to the act of the Great Dragon, Tragor."

That's who Tragor is, Iviana realized. She remembered now when he had awoken her on the dusty wilderness floor, but recalled little more of their journey beyond that.

"The council requests your presence in a formal meeting tomorrow afternoon," the ageless lady continued, then waited, but Iviana was uncertain what was expected of her. "Do you consent?" the woman queried with eyebrow raised.

Iviana grew redder still, then nodded.

The woman granted Iviana an austere smile before turning her attention to the audience. "I encourage you all to introduce yourselves to our young visitor," she paused before adding with the tiniest hint of a smirk, "She will not bite."

The crowd responded with hesitant laughter and the woman gestured for the musical group to begin again.

Next thing Iviana knew, Nimua was tugging at her sleeve.

Iviana turned. "Huh?"

"You can sit down now."

Iviana did so, readily, and barely had time to recuperate before the islanders began crowding around her, wanting to see the stranger and to introduce themselves. Some were exceptionally warm and welcoming, some only stared and smiled and listened to her answer others' questions, while others glared from afar. Iviana was not offered the chance to notice this, however.

"How did you meet Tragor?" the questioning began and continued."You must have been the one to heal his wound!"—murmurs—"She must have the gift!"—"Impossible. Don't be daft."—"How did you get so ill?"—"How old are you, girl?"—"How long will you be staying?"—"I like your hair."

Iviana was pelted with comments and questions until, enough of the people had fulfilled their curiosity and others were able to live vicariously through what was being spoken about her amid the crowd until eventually the uncomfortable ordeal ended.

Nimua patted Iviana's arm as the last of the crowd left them. "It's almost time!" she exclaimed.

"Time for what?"

"What I told you about!"

Iviana was about to ask to be reminded when she heard a loud whistling followed with an even louder explosion of light and color bursting in the sky above them. All of the sudden, there were hundreds of colored stars exploding all around over head and off in the distance. "How are you doing this?" she asked Nimua, thoroughly awed by the show.

"Oh, don't be silly. I'm not doing it all myself. Haven't you ever seen fireworks?"

"No." Iviana responded, still awed. "How did you get them so far away?"

"Oh, those are the other islands. They're all acknowledging your presence. When one island has a celebration, generally all the islands follow suit. So when my mother and I decided we were going to do something special for you, everyone else had to do it too."

"Even though not everyone believes your presence should be cause for celebration," Darist cut in.

Nimua elbowed the young man in the stomach.

"What do you mean?" Iviana was alarmed. She hadn't thought she may not be welcome among these strangers, "kin" or not.

"Forget about it, Ivi. Enjoy the show," Nimua

123

said, smiling reassuringly, but Iviana could see the concern hiding behind her twinkling eyes.

❧ II ❧

"HURRY, IVI," Nimua urged the next morning.

Iviana pulled a soft pink tunic over her head and layered it with a flowing white toga. The clothes had been laid out for her sometime before she awoke, though she could not say when.

"I think Darist is waiting outside. He told me last night he wanted to join us," Nimua finished.

Iviana pulled a belt around her waist and attempted to fasten it. "I'm trying. These clothes are so peculiar." She growled and gave up on it.

"Let me." It took Nimua only a moment to fasten it.

Iviana eyed her.

"I've had much more practice," Nimua explained with a smile.

They headed out the door and were greeted by Darist.

"Now, where to start," Nimua thought aloud.

"The Grand Pavilion, of course. She hasn't seen it in the daylight yet," Darist spoke matter-of-factly.

"Mmm, that's dull. I say we take her to the dragon's lair. That way she can see a familiar face."

"How do you know how familiar his face is to her?" Darist queried. "For all you know he picked her up while she was unconscious and dragged her here."

Nimua glared at him. "I just know. He looked really concerned when we took her from him. Why would he feel concern for a mere stranger... let alone break the rules to bring her here?"

"He *looked* concerned?" Darist teased. "How can you tell when a dragon looks concerned, Nimua?"

"*Some* of us are intuitive," Nimua snapped.

Iviana broke in before the banter could continue. "I have known him for a little while... if you mean my dragon, that is," she supplied.

They turned to her, almost surprised to find her there.

"Of course," Nimua agreed with a smile. "You said last night you rescued him from some man. What was his name? Flynn. He sounds wretched. But it's so exciting you can use a sword. And *you* rescued *Tragor*."

"He's really not wretched at all once you get to

know him." Iviana felt she needed to explain. "He was just desperate because, well, he..." She didn't understand why she felt uncomfortable telling them why he'd wanted the heart. Fortunately, she didn't have to explain.

"You got acquainted with that reprobate?" Darist asked, almost accusingly.

"Well, yes," Iviana admitted. "He saved my life actually... and I saved his."

Darist didn't look convinced it had been such a good idea, but Nimua was of an opposite opinion.

"You saved each other's lives?" she gushed. "How romantic."

"Yes, about as romantic as she and the dragon saving one other..." Darist put in.

He was rewarded with a glower from Nimua.

"Oh, no, it wasn't like that," Iviana tried to explain. "It just happened. We kept running into one another somehow and–"

"You kept running into each other?" Nimua asked thoughtfully. "That's interesting..."

"More like he was following you," Darist retorted.

Iviana smiled as she remembered the time she'd accused Flynn of the same thing. It *was* odd they kept crossing paths.

The three had traveled around a jaggedly-cut cliff of dark gray limestone when what appeared before them made Iviana gasp. The bright green island grass she'd been enjoying beneath her feet led into an emerald valley overflowing with dragons. She had noticed some of them flying overhead that morning and had even seen some out her windows while confined to her bed, but she'd never seen so many at once or guessed so many still existed. Here in this valley, the graceful creatures were breathtaking. Some were lounging and grazing while others circled overhead.

Suddenly, a shadow fell over the three and before Iviana knew it, a pale blue and green dragon appeared on the ground before her.

Iviana ran to her dragon and held him about the neck, stroking his back.

"Your name is Tragor, huh?"

She turned to Nimua and Darist and found them frozen where they stood.

"What's wrong?" she asked them, bewildered.

Nimua answered quietly, "You just embraced Tragor, the *Great* Dragon of the Ages."

Iviana looked into the dragon's eyes. He was amused.

"Well, looks like he has a new favorite," Darist

commented, rousing from his stupor.

"A new what?" Iviana asked.

"He hasn't let anyone near him since the Age of the Great One. That's almost a hundred years past, when we and the dragons fought against the evil that linked our worlds," Darist explained.

"What are you talking about?" Iviana asked.

"It's really too much to go into now. Lets just say, you're no Latos."

Nimua punched Darist in the arm. "You don't know that! She saved the *life* of the Great Dragon. I think that makes her fantastic, personally."

"You'd really compare her to *Latos* because she did one heroic deed?"

"She saved that Flynn's life as well and I bet there are a thousand things we don't know about her, right Ivi?"

"Who's Latos?" Iviana inquired impatiently.

Nimua continued, "Besides, *Darist*, it's really not up to us. It's up to Tragor."

The three turned to Tragor who seemed to shrug. He then turned to Iviana and gestured toward his back as if inviting her to climb on.

"Oh, I really shouldn't," Iviana responded. "I'm in the middle of a tour."

The Great Dragon of the Ages stamped his front

legs in a tantrum and glanced to his back again.

Iviana giggled and hopped on. "I'm sorry!" she called to Nimua and Darist as she and Tragor gracefully rose into the air. "I'll meet you later!" With that, the dragon soared into the sky.

As Tragor flew her over every inch of the island, Iviana discovered the view from above was even more beautiful. When at last Tragor rounded back to where they had begun their flight, he raced higher into the sky above them, barely allowing Iviana time to brace herself.

"Stop showing off!" she screamed at him as he continued to ascend.

At last, they broke through the clouds and all around was white, terrifying and glorious at once. Iviana embraced her surroundings, running her hands through the fluffy white clouds and wondering if anyone had ever experienced the view she was enjoying.

Without warning, Tragor swooped beneath the clouds once again and the sight of dozens upon dozens of islands spread further than her eyes could see. From the little time she'd been in the realm, it had never been made clear that the Greater Archipelagos were so expansive, but here was this intensely blue ocean covered in countless green islands. She found herself wishing she was an artist so she could capture the scene forever. Though, she knew, even if she could, there was no way anyone would understand how immaculate it was without seeing the view for themselves. And then she wondered how many *had* seen it. She doubted she was the only person to have flown with a dragon.

Tragor flew her nearer some of the islands whose inhabitants stared up at the pair with curious expressions, but carried on with whatever they were doing. Iviana had a sudden desire to visit some of these islands and wondered if she was ever going to be granted the chance.

All at once, Tragor jerked to a halt and they were left floating in mid-air. Turning his head back the way they had come as though he had heard something, he immediately dashed back to the Isle of Dragons and dropped her before the largest building she had seen since she'd been there. Naii rushed up to her, informing she was late.

"Late for what?" Iviana asked with some anxiety.

Naii lowered her voice, "Your meeting with the council."

Iviana had completely forgotten her appointment and struggled to believe it was already time. "It's not supposed to be until this afternoon!"

CASSANDRA BOYSON

she declared.

"Iviana, dear, it's past the noon meal. I was looking for you everywhere until Nimua told me you went off with Tragor."

Iviana's stomach dropped. She couldn't believe they had been gone so long. It did explain why she was so hungry, but there was no time to worry about that. Naii took her by the arm and hurried her up the stairs of the big building, over the terrace and through the door where she was encircled by a number of intimidating individuals in tall, marble chairs.

Naii gave her a smile as if to convey everything would be alright and went to take her own seat among the council. This left Iviana standing alone in the center of the marble-floored room, with all eyes on her. Her face flushed crimson.

The ageless woman who'd welcomed her at the banquet the night before spoke in her booming voice, "Iviana, thank you for joining us. Can we provide a seat for our young guest?"

Iviana was pleased with the idea of being moved from the center of the room to one of the chairs encircling, but before she knew it, a chair was pulled up behind her. She forced herself to thank the gentleman who'd brought it for her.

"Firstly," the woman began, "I would like to introduce myself and the rest of the council. I am Rhimesh, Realm Leader of the of the Greater Archipelagos. To my left, Kurnin." She gestured to a man whose looks Iviana did not care for, though she couldn't say why. "He is the leader of this island—the northern-most island and our capitol: the Isle of Dragons." She continued around the room until Iviana knew the names of each council member present. All had some position of authority within the Isle of Dragons, excluding three. These were from some other islands whose names Iviana knew she would never remember.

"Now, there are a number of matters we must discuss today," Rhimesh continued, "and we would like to do so in your presence, as they are concerning yourself. Firstly, we would like to hear what you know of your parents. What knowledge do you already possess about the Greater Archipelagos? How did you come to know the Great Dragon of the Ages?"

Iviana nervously cleared her throat and tried to focus all her attention on the intimidating Realm Leader. This did not help. Eyes cast to the floor, she began, "I know very little, I'm afraid. It is my understanding that, after I was born, I was left with my mentor, Naphtali—"

"*Who* did she say?" the man named Kurnin interrupted. There were murmurs about the room.

"Let the girl finish," Rhimesh demanded and silence fell once again.

Iviana touched her hands to her face in an attempt to cool it and continued, "I can tell you she taught me everything she knew. If you wish to know the closest person I had to a mother, it is—was—it was her."

Iviana paused and Rhimesh took the opportunity to ask, "If you will permit my asking, did Naphtali not tell you anything more about your parents?"

"No," Iviana replied. "I lived my whole life with Naphtali. I learned to heal. That is how I met my dragon—Tragor, I mean. I can't perfectly explain how I came upon him; I was not searching for him. A man attacked him and attempted to slay him. He nearly succeeded, but I was able to use the healing that Naphtali taught me to save the dragon.

Murmurs began and grew louder until Rhimesh hushed them with a slight movement of her hands. "This could mean a number of things," she said to them. "Please continue, Iviana."

Iviana did so. "As for prior knowledge of this

land, I did not know it existed until I came to a door in a place called Jaela's Cavern."

Rhimesh raised her eyebrows in surprise and asked, "Naphtali told you nothing of us?"

"No."

"Please explain more about the time you spent with Naphtali. She taught you healing, you claim?"

"Yes, she did. We kept to ourselves, mostly, but others would come to her for healing and she taught me what she knew. We lived in a small cottage. We tended the garden. She taught me how to defend myself with a sword and... I'm sorry, I really don't know what else to tell you. We lived very simply."

"How much do you know about healing, child?"

Iviana thought a moment. "The day before she died, she told me she was satisfied with what I knew—that she had nothing more to teach me—that my gift was my own and I must use it as I see fit."

This time the murmurs contained shouts of disbelief. Some accused Iviana of lying about everything. Others said she was just like her father and grandfather. They ignored Rhimesh when she tried to silence them. Iviana turned to Naii whose eyes normally looked like serene pools of purple water. Instead, they were inflamed with rage.

Naii stood from her chair and shouted as Iviana

could never have imagined she was able. *"Silence!"* she demanded.

The murmurs slowly ceased. The council members recognized the passion that the grounded woman conveyed was not at all usual for her. Naii looked to Rhimesh for permission to speak and Rhimesh consented.

"We all know the Great Gifts like to appear where no one expects. If you'll remember the historic texts, Latos shared the gifts were sent from the Great One, his Friend. From the past, we know the Great One has never been anything but absolutely correct. I think we've all guessed the parentage of this young woman and though her grandfather may have thrown away his gift, his granddaughter has been given a chance at another, one of the rarest and one that is always greatly needed. I do not doubt Iviana's word. I believe we should honor Naphtali in that, at least."

When she finished, one of the council released a "Here, here." Some nodded in agreement while others appeared torn. Kurnin, leader of the island, was red with anger, though Iviana couldn't begin to understand his reaction.

Rhimesh spoke to Iviana, "That is all we need from you for now. You are excused."

Iviana hesitated. She did not want to be dismissed—not before she learned who her parents were—and she had the feeling they were about to discuss her fate as a healer. She wanted to listen for that as well. "But I –" she began to say, but Naii gave a short jerk of her head in warning and waved the girl out.

Once outside, Iviana released a long, anguished sigh. She didn't know what she had expected, but it hadn't been that.

"How did it go?" Nimua rose from a bench on the terrace and went to her friend.

"I don't know," Iviana answered. "It didn't feel like it went well."

"You never know with them, though," Nimua comforted. "They can change their minds in an instant and they hardly ever agree completely on anything anyway. Majority rules and it helps that you have my mother."

"I think they would have eaten me alive had she not stepped in."

"She likes you, and not just because Naphtali was her mother."

Iviana jumped involuntarily. "What?" she squeaked, remembering the day she had informed Naii of Naphtali's death and the tears that Naii had shed.

"Oh, she hasn't told you?" Nimua looked caught. "Well, she likes to think things through thoroughly before speaking about them. She would have told you in time."

Iviana closed her eyes. "My life used to be so simple."

Nimua was uncertain how to respond. Her life had been simple as well—too simple—and she had felt completely bored with it until Iviana arrived.

"You need to meet Marquen," Nimua decided.

As she suddenly raced away, Iviana had no choice but to follow.

It's nice to have a friend, Iviana thought with a grin on her face as she went.

They walked near the path they had taken to visit Tragor at the dragon's lair, but continued forward to begin hiking one of the tallest formations on the island.

"Surely this is not really called Seer's *Hill?"* Iviana asked. "It's a mountain."

Nimua skipped along the incline. "Maybe you just need more exercise."

"Or maybe I'm just not used to mountain climbing," Iviana panted, holding her side. "How much further?"

"Oh, not much. You see that fog up above?"

"Yes."

"Well, it's a while beyond that."

Iviana stumbled. "You're kidding."

"Unless you pick up the pace, we won't get there before nightfall."

"Alright. Lets just..." Iviana sat herself on a nearby rock. "...take a little breather."

"Fine. Drink this." Nimua pulled a small container of water from a pocket at her side.

Iviana drank it and immediately felt strengthened. Holding the bottle to her face, she examined its contents.

"What's in this water?" she asked.

"Nothing. Why?"

"I feel stronger."

"Oh, yes. Water does that. Doesn't yours?"

"I suppose... but not that quickly." She drank the rest of the liquid. "Lets go," Iviana sang, jumping to her feet.

Eventually the young women came upon a rustic brown cabin amidst the fog. It was covered with greenery and surrounded with an enormous array of vegetation. The garden flourished even more than Iviana and Naphtali's garden at home, and they'd worked on it for as long as she could remember.

"It's not white," Iviana commented in astonishment. Everything on the island that had been man-made had been some shade of white. It had almost been overwhelming.

"Yes?" Nimua raised a brow and knocked on the door.

"Enter!" a man's voice called.

Nimua turned the knob to reveal a man with a thick brown beard who appeared a little older than the women.

He smiled and greeted them. "Ah, Nimua, I knew you'd be by sometime soon." He turned to Iviana. "Hello, Ivi."

"Uh, hello. You're Marquen?" Iviana asked.

"Yes, of course. Please, have a seat." He motioned toward two chairs pulled out on the other side of a rustic table.

"You built another chair," Nimua stated before taking a seat.

Marquen smiled hugely behind his bushy beard, "I couldn't have Ivi sitting on the ground now could I? She would think my manners ill. Therefore, I would have to sit on the ground myself. I don't care for wooden floors."

"How were you so sure I would come?" Iviana

asked curiously.

"He's a Seer, Ivi," Nimua replied as though it should be obvious.

"Mm, yes," Marquen agreed, "but that doesn't mean I know everything. I'm not *Latos*..." His eyes sparkled in a smile. "...but I am pretty close."

"Well, aren't we chesty today?" Nimua teased.

"Not so, not so. I simply speak as I see it," the man defended himself good-naturedly.

Iviana looked him over as he spoke, thinking he seemed centuries older than he appeared. She tried to reason why. Was it the beard?

She also wished she knew what his being a "Seer" meant.

"What are you thinking so hard about, friend?" Marquen asked her.

"I, uh..." Iviana's mind raced, searching for any answer other than the truth. "I wonder why you only had two chairs before and why you live so far from everyone else."

"He's a hermit," Nimua supplied for him.

"I don't think you could say that exactly," Marquen replied. "'Hermit' implies that I am a person living in solitude. 'Solitude' implies that I dwell in a lonely place. I am neither lonely or alone."

"Picky," Nimua murmured.

Without warning, a white blur flew in through the window.

"Ah, here is one of the two visitors I receive who keep me from becoming lonesome."

Iviana's attention was caught by the white bird now perched on Marquen's shoulder. "Hey! That's my—I mean, that's the dove... I keep seeing," Iviana ended cautiously. She had not meant to burst out so.

"Yes, he confirmed the vision I had of you coming to the island."

Vision, Iviana thought. She was beginning to understand what they meant by Seer.

"Alright," Nimua interrupted. "I know I'm your only visitor, but do you really have to resort to birds as a means of company?"

"He's not just a bird," Iviana corrected in a dreamy tone as she looked into the eyes of the dove.

"Mm, 'Intuitive Ivi'," Marquen singsonged as he stroked the dove's wing. "What else can you see?" he asked her.

"What do you mean?" Iviana inquired.

"I'm not sure," he answered. "I think you'll know in time, if I'm correct."

Nimua broke in, "We're here because Ivi went before the council today and she doesn't feel very good about it. I hoped you could help her feel better, as you do for me."

"What happened?" the man asked, ready to listen.

"Well, they..." Iviana wavered, "they wanted me to tell them about myself."

"That sounds simple enough," the Seer said. He smirked before adding, "But I doubt the council allowed it to be so."

"I did as they asked and when I told them I was a... a healer, they seemed to become somewhat disturbed by it. Then I was dismissed and I'm... afraid they're going to tell me that I can't heal anymore. It's the most precious thing I have right now. It's who I am and what Naphtali gave me." Iviana hadn't realized before what her true fears were concerning the meeting, but as she sat facing Marquen, her twisted, confused thoughts seemed to unravel.

Marquen looked straight into Iviana's bright blue eyes a moment and Iviana had the uncanny feeling that what he was about to say could quite possibly change her life.

Finally, he uttered something meaningfully, but it was in a tongue she did not understand.

The room was silent a moment.

"What?" Iviana asked him, perplexed.

"Decide your own fate, Ivi... Make an earthquake."

His words settled over her like the first, silent snowfall of winter, then plunged deep into her heart like a knife. She did not ask him what he meant. She felt he would not answer her if she did. Its true meaning was something for her to decipher.

Make an earthquake. It was not a dream—a lofty idea out in space somewhere. It was a command—a command that she understood completely and not at all, and it came with a presence she couldn't quite grasp... *Make an earthquake.*

She thought on those words as Nimua led her out the door and while they made their way down the path that led to where the rest of the islanders lived and continued to dwell on them through dinner until Nimua and Darist drew her out. The longer she thought on them, the more the words revolutionized her reality. Before, she had been merely trying to survive, but now she had purpose and design... even if she wasn't certain of the details.

After the meal, Iviana excused herself and made her way toward the beach. The water was golden with the sunset this night as she waded idly through the ankle-deep water on the shore. She found a miniature island of dark gray rock and sat upon it.

144

Knees folded up within her arms, she rested her chin on them and looked out at the golden sky. Shades of pink and amber were cast across the sea line and she could make out the dark image of a nearby island.

While she'd been in the meeting with the council, she had seen a map beyond Rhimesh's head. It contained every island in the Greater Archipelagos and listed the names of each. She doubted she could ever learn even half of them and wondered if she would ever visit any. When it came down to it, she didn't know what she was doing here or how long she would stay... or how long she would be permitted to stay.

Though she was supposed to be of the same blood as the islanders, it was apparent many of them did not trust her. Whatever her parents had done, had been, had cast a shadow on who she was. She really didn't think it fair, especially considering she didn't have a single memory of them. The islanders knew of Naphtali too. She didn't know if that was good or bad, but the bit about her having been taught healing sounded like it could be a problem. If it was, she didn't know why. Maybe they simply had a problem with the fact that she was given the chance at healing and they felt she didn't deserve it. Perhaps they would rather she not possess the knowledge at all. When she had been dismissed, she felt they were going to decide her fate... but like Marquen had insinuated... her fate was hers to control, not theirs. After all, she barely knew these people.

When she was seven, she had seen Naphtali fixing an ointment for a cut.

"Naphtali," she had said, "I want to do that."

Naphtali had smiled and replied, "We'll see."

What had she meant exactly? Was it that she wasn't certain she wanted to teach her or that it wasn't up to her at all, but a higher being? A higher being... that was something she had never thought much about before. She wondered if it would be the same being in both Kaern and the Greater Archipelagos or if each world had its own.

The issue of her being in another realm was something else entirely. What did that even mean? Could it really be true? She had a rough memory of her trip to the Greater Archipelagos. They had traveled through... something... She didn't know what to call it. Perhaps she'd dreamed it. Even so, there had been references to such things as other realms, worlds or dimensions, but most was speculation and met with cynicism.

If only someone would answer my questions, she thought silently.

"Are the sunsets any different in your world?" a voice broke into her thoughts.

Iviana looked back, but recognized the voice before she saw him.

"They're fairly similar, but they don't feel so close there. Here, it's so big it feels like it could be sitting in my lap."

"Mm, I never thought of it that way." Darist paused, then continued, "I heard you caused a commotion in the council today... not that, that is difficult to do."

"They're not very trusting, are they? I mean, do I seem dangerous to you?" Iviana asked him.

She saw a smirk appear on his face as he stood beside her. "Sort of. Everything about you is unexpected and everything about life here is pretty much the same... all day... everyday. You have no idea how happy Nimua is to have you here... or Naii and myself." There was silence for a few minutes until Darist asked what he'd been wanting to. "Are you happy to be here?"

It took her just as long to answer as it had taken him to ask. "Before I came here and after Naphtali died, I felt like I was going to be undone with loneliness. I had no one. I'm happy not to be alone."

Silence followed for a long while before Darist

said, "I think you'll fit in after a while and be accepted. Especially with your healing gift. You could really do a lot of good."

Iviana hesitated. "I don't know that I want to fit in here," she admitted.

Her reply took him off guard. "Then you don't like it here?" he asked.

"No, I do... I think I do. It's just, I want to be accepted as I am... not who I could become."

"Mmm... you're right. These people aren't very changing though, Ivi."

"So I am to be an outcast forever?" she asked hopelessly.

"You're not an outcast now... you're just not... trusted by everyone. Not yet, anyway."

Iviana nodded. "Thank you for being honest. I think Nimua tries to cushion everything for me. I prefer to know where things stand."

They were both thoughtful for a while as it grew dark. "I guess I should be getting back. They don't like people out too late," Darist warned.

"Of course not."

Darist laughed. "Alright, you sleep well. Tell me what you think of the blue fish tomorrow."

"What?"

"Nothing." He smiled. "Good nigh-"

"Wait..." Iviana stopped him. "Promise me you'll tell me about the Age of the Great One tomorrow—and Latos?"

"Nimua would kill me if I beat her to it."

"Then she can tell me or you both can. I don't care. I just want a promise that I'll be told."

"Alright, I promise."

Iviana had so many more questions and that may have even been the least of what she wanted to know, but she was happy for the hope of even the smallest ounce of understanding. How could they expect her to go about life here if she was never to be told the truth about anything? She was sick of her questions being ignored as if she were a small child with too much curiosity. She would not be treated like a small child. Naphtali wanted better for her than that and she would find some place where someone would see her for what she was and could live in peace with only that. If these people couldn't accept her, if they wanted her to leave, that was fine. She would be fine.

Well, it was time for sleep. She stepped off her rock and as her foot touched the water, she noticed something shimmer next to it. Suddenly, one by one and two by two, numerous blue glowing things appeared within the water until the sea was shimmering blue under the silver of the moon. These must be the blue fish, she thought with a sigh.

This place was full of beautiful surprises.

ഇ12ഔ

IVIANA WAS STANDING by the ocean's edge when she felt a pain on the left side of her body and could no longer hold herself up. After falling upon the shore, she looked to the side of her body where she'd felt the jolt of pain... and there was nothing there. Half of her was missing. She couldn't get up or shout for help.

A woman came up from the ocean and started toward her. "Ah, right where I need you, my dear," her cold voice spoke. The woman from the ocean snapped her fingers and a fire flashed to life beside Iviana. Shapes formed within the flames, grasping for her half flesh. They burned her, but she couldn't get away.

Please, stop them! she cried desperately in her mind, unable to speak it.

The woman heard her thoughts and laughed

madly. "It is what you deserve, daughter of Latos. You will share his fate."

You're mistaken. I am not his daughter! Iviana screamed in her mind as a flame gripped her ankle.

"I am rarely ever mistaken, foolish girl," the woman answered lightly.

The flame began to crawl up Iviana's leg, over her half stomach, reaching for her half heart and then she awoke with a start. She was breathing hard and sweating as if in response to the dream-flames.

"Daughter of Latos," she whispered aloud, quickly throwing off her covers and dressing. She was going to get some answers.

&

"Nimua, where's your mother?" Iviana asked when Nimua answered the door. "I need to speak with her right away."

"I'm sorry, Ivi. She's not here. Why? Are you alright?"

"Yes, I just have some questions."

"Oh, well, she's visiting another island for the next day or so. Can I answer anything for you?"

Iviana hesitated. "No, I don't think so. I just..."

Suddenly Iviana noticed Nimua's attire. "What are you wearing?"

Nimua blushed. "It was my mother's wedding frock and Naphtali's before her. I was just... trying it."

Iviana touched the delicate fabric. "It's lovely. It really is... oh, are you—are you getting married?"

"No!" Nimua blushed again. "Well, yes. Someday, I suppose. I just like to try it on sometimes."

"Ah... do you have anyone in mind?" Iviana smirked, following Nimua into her home. "Darist?"

Nimua's eyes grew wide. "No! Are you joking? He's like an annoying brother I've never been able to rid myself of. I guess when we were children we liked each other, but we've outgrown that, thank heaven."

"Ah. Well, it's a beautiful dress." Iviana paused, then added, "You'd kill each other anyway."

They laughed at that. "Are you kidding? I'd kill him before we even made it to the alter." They were both tearing with laughter. "He'd want to carry me around everywhere to show off his biceps!"

When they were able to settle themselves, Nimua removed the wedding attire, saying, "You know what would be fun? We should find someone for *you.*"

"Please, no." Iviana hadn't had much experience with romance, but she had taken a fancy to a young man when she was twelve. It hadn't gone well.

"Come *on!* It'd give me something to do. Besides, I'm known for my successful match-making," Nimua said with a wink.

Iviana wasn't at all tempted. "Oh, please. I would *really* rather you not. If you need something to do..." she searched for something to distract the girl, "we'll go flying."

"Flying!" Nimua jumped up. "I'm not supposed to! I mean, I've never–"

"You've never or it's not aloud?"

"I just don't care to tamper with the dragons. That's for adventurers and people with the Great Gifts."

"Hm. What are these Great Gifts, anyway?"

"There are a number of them. There are the Healers, like yourself, and those with special strength—I think we know who was blessed with that feat—and there are those who can breathe underwater—Swimmers—and some can sense danger. Actually, some can sense much more than that: the Seers, like Marquen. They receive word from the Great One in pictures. Then there are

Seekers, Inventors, Benders and—"

"Wait," Iviana interrupted. "Some of you can breathe underwater? That's..." She couldn't find a word.

"Well, all the Great Gifts are impressive, especially those that are rare, like yours." Her face shadowed a bit before she continued, "There are also those who have no Great Gift at all."

They were quiet a moment as what Nimua was implying set in Iviana's mind. "Well, does... does hospitality count?" Iviana asked. "'Cause you've got that in abundance."

Nimua chuckled. "I guess it does now," she answered sarcastically.

"You said their are Healers?" Iviana said thoughtfully. "Like me? What makes one a Healer? How is it a 'Great Gift'?"

"Great Gifts are from the Great One. He anoints individuals with them."

"The Great One?"

Nimua raised her brows in surprise. "You don't know who the Great One is?"

Iviana shook her head. "Never heard of Him."

"Hm." Nimua looked her over. "There is no... no Great One spoken of in Kierelia or in any part of your world? Naphtali never said anything?"

"Not that I know of. Who is He, Nimua?"

"Well, He's... He's hard to explain. He created the Greater Archipelagos. He created all things—even your land and those living there, from what I understand. He created us and He gifts some of us with certain attributes: the Great Gifts. Your healing came from Him."

"Why would He give me a Great Gift? I don't understand. I thought I learned healing from Naphtali."

"Well, I don't know much about it personally, but I'm sure there are aspects of it that can be learned. However, there's a certain power one has, to will the healing to happen. I've heard something about a glow."

Iviana nodded. The glow: she'd seen that before, but she had always assumed it was in her mind. "But how could He even know who I am?"

Nimua struggled. "Like I said, He's hard to explain. I guess I don't know Who He is in your world, but here, He's everything to us... and He knows all."

"Can I meet Him?"

Nimua giggled. "It's doubtful. He's the Great One, the Creator. I've never met anyone who has, but who's to say it's impossible."

This explanation only confused Iviana more. Why couldn't she see Him? Why wouldn't He want to see those He'd created? Why create people in the first place? She didn't understand Him and she wasn't certain she believed in Him.

Iviana shook her head. She didn't want to think about such things now. Remembering what they had been talking about before, she said, "You live on an island full of dragons and you've never flown before?"

Nimua nodded.

"Then *why* are we sitting here gabbing? We're going to visit Tragor, whether you like it or not."

❦

"Alright, I feel like the most ignorant person in the Greater Archipelagos," Nimua admitted after they dismounted Tragor. "I can't believe I've never done that before!"

Tragor's eyes were lit, as though satisfied Nimua had enjoyed herself. It had taken a fair amount of time to draw Nimua near enough to him that she might get on his back and longer still to get her to stop screaming once they were in the air. That was when Tragor had made up his mind he would win her over by showing her a wonderful time. His efforts had been successful.

Iviana giggled at her friend. "Neither can I," she said, then asked more seriously, "What held you back?"

"I don't know exactly... I suppose I felt undeserving; like it wasn't my place? You'd be surprised how many of us have never experienced it."

"You're all mad then." Iviana put her hands to her head in frustration and disbelief. "There's so much beauty here; so much you take for granted."

Nimua shrugged. "Yes, but I bet you could say the same for those in your land."

Iviana blinked, then nodded. "You're right," she said. Then she looked about her. "Where are we going?" She had been following Nimua the moment they landed without questioning their destination.

Nimua smirked. "I've got something to show you now."

They made their way down to a part of the beach Iviana had never seen before—except perhaps momentarily from the sky—where there was a group of islanders swimming and playing in the water.

"What're we doing here?" Iviana asked.

Nimua worked to keep the smile off her face. "Remember when I told you about the people who can breathe underwater?"

Iviana gave her full attention. "Yes."

"This is where they like to spend their time."

Iviana gasped and studied some of the young Swimmers who were there. They didn't look different from anyone else. "So... so we'll get to see it in action??"

Nimua smiled with sparkling eyes. "Sure."

They strolled to where the calm water met the sand on the beach. "Nico!" Nimua called to a young, blonde man who waved to her and started toward them. Nimua turned to Iviana and explained, "That's my cousin, Nico."

"Hello, ladies," the young man greeted. "What brings you to this end of the island?"

Nimua's bright smile appeared again. "I was hoping Ivi and I could swim with you all for a bit."

"Aah, I see," Nico smiled with understanding. "It'd be a pleasure." He called to a beautiful Swimmer name Brenna with deeply tanned skin and honey-blonde hair. Once she'd joined them, he asked, "Would you mind finding these ladies some suits?"

The brilliant Brenna echoed the smiles surrounding Iviana. "Your first swim?"

Iviana was confused by their demeanor. "Uh, well, not really. I used to go swimming in the stream near my home all the time."

Brenna's dazzling smile grew larger. "Alright, lets get you changed then."

Brenna led them to a small building where she presented them with something lighter to wear while they swam. When she left them alone to change, Iviana raised an eyebrow at Nimua and asked, "What's going on?"

"What do you mean?" Nimua asked innocently.

"I don't understand all the smiling."

Nimua tried to be coy, but gave in. "Alright, there's something I didn't mention about the Swimmers earlier. It's not just that they can breathe underwater, but they can also pass on the gift momentarily to anyone they're touching. It's actually how we travel from island to island most of the time. Gets pretty tiring, but it's not bad."

Iviana, having just put on her suit, dropped her clothes to the floor.

Nimua couldn't help but laugh. "Well, say something! I'll call the Healer otherwise."

"How is that possible?" Iviana asked in a tone obviously trying to contain her amazement.

"Sheesh, I don't know. It's just a part of the gift

to be able to share it with others."

"But how..."

"Oh, just come on." Nimua took her hand and led her down to the shoreline.

"You ready?" Nico called as they approached.

Iviana nodded, still a little awed. She was trying to imagine what it was going to be like.

"You did explain it to her then?" he asked Nimua.

"Yes, and she's not quite over it yet. I'm afraid we'll have to take her in as is."

"Alright," Nico turned to Iviana and held out his arm, "if you'll just take my hand, we'll head in."

Iviana reached for the hand he offered, but hesitated. "What if it doesn't work?" she asked.

Nico grinned. "It will. I promise."

The moment they dove beneath the water, it was blue magic all around. Iviana gasped in wonder at what she saw, then gasped again. *I really* can *breathe underwater,* she thought. It was a strange sensation, but tolerable. A thought occurred to her that maybe she could speak underwater as well, but when she attempted it, tiny bubbles floated up around her like a glimmering symphony of stars dancing from her mouth. Nico, Nimua and Brenna looked as though they'd be laughing at her if they could.

Nico made a gesture to the girls and pulled Iviana—Nimua and Brenna following—further out to sea where a colorful reef revealed itself like the fireworks from a few nights before. The rock was covered with coral in blues, oranges, purples and greens, with various creatures swimming about, not the least bit phased by the humans' presence. There were fish with large foreheads and beaked teeth grazing off the coral while turtles lounged on the reef. Iviana discovered the reason for this when a school of colorful fish began nibbling at the surface of the turtles. Nico later explained this was how the turtles were able to rid themselves of the algae collected on their shells.

The reef showed scarring from the grazing fish, but she could tell that, in the lushness of these waters, the corals would grow back swiftly. Indeed, this was an underwater oasis, a dynamic abundance of living entities. As they paused their swimming to watch the scene, Iviana breathed, her bright blue eyes sparkling with emotion. With the sun gleaming down in a tunnel of light around her, she felt as though she could remain within the extents of this ocean forever. As she enjoyed her surroundings, a love washed over her that she couldn't comprehend. She felt like someone had created this wonderful scene just for her, that these waters were a token of affection for her to enjoy. This was how she often felt while leisurely walking in the forest at home, but in this unique place, with the ocean water pressing around her, the feelings were intensified.

Nico stole her away to view another scene made up of a shimmering wall of fish, moving even more gracefully than her dragon. They were of one mind and purpose, totally united. Their movements reminded her of the dancers she'd seen perform at dinner the night before.

Below them, Nico pointed out a breathtaking array of sandy-colored snake-like creatures which he told her later were garden eels. It truly was a garden of living creatures that would smoothly rise and retreat as needed, never removing their tales from the sand. Iviana wished she could glide about life as these creatures did, but perhaps that was not what humans were created for. At least she didn't have to live her whole life stuck in the sand. She could fly and explore wherever her heart desired and she realized that she hadn't yet appreciated the complete freedom she possessed until now.

Suddenly, they were slicing threw the water with the ocean surroundings surging past them, all the while Iviana was being tugged along by Nico. She was surprised at what a powerful swimmer he was, but supposed, with his wonderful gift, he probably spent every free moment in this underwater world. He slowed as they reached a sandbar and loosed his grip on Iviana's hand. Immediately, she lost the ability to breathe within the water and rose to her feet on the sand where the water reached her waist. She was about to gleefully shout to Nimua when she noticed the strange animals swimming with the four of them.

She hesitated, saying, "Uuum... what are those?" Raising her arms out of the water, she scooted her leg away from one that was coming near her.

"They're stingrays," Nico answered matter-of-factly.

"*Sting*rays?" Iviana mumbled.

The one that had been coming toward her began lapping its wings up against her like a puppy excited to see her. Others joined in. Iviana released a small yelp and tried to get away.

"They just want to be fed," Nico assured her.

"Oh, *that* makes me feel better!" Iviana replied in a high, shaky voice.

"No, no, no," he said, chuckling. "Here." He held out a handful of food that came from a pouch at his side. When he dropped the food in the water, the stingrays let her be and hurried over to what he provided.

"See?" he said innocently.

Another of the stingrays swam near her, but this one was much calmer and kept itself at a small distance, allowing Iviana to admire it without feeling threatened.

"You should try touching her," Nico suggested.

Iviana made a face at him, but when she drew her gaze back to the stingray, she was overcome with curiosity. Slowly, carefully, she reached her hand toward it. At first touch, she immediately pulled back. "It—it's slimy," she said shakily.

"Not really. Try again."

She obeyed, rubbing the ray more slowly this time, refusing to scare. As she ran her hand from head to tale, it was silky smooth, but when she moved the opposite direction, it was rough and scratchy.

She made a face and Nico guessed, "It's rough, eh? It's because of how the flesh is constructed. We believe it helps them swim."

The ray she was petting swished its tale back and forth, but remained in place.

"She likes you," Nico commented.

"Does she have a name?"

He let out a small, half chuckle. "You think I can keep track of every stingray in the ocean? I actually don't even know if it's male or female."

"Oh. Well, I'm naming her Serena."

"I see. Because she's so calm?"

Iviana nodded.

"It's probably because she's been well fed already."

"I don't think so," Iviana insisted.

The young man shrugged. "Suit yourself."

Iviana turned to where Nimua was, a few feet away from her. "This is... amazing," she said breathlessly.

Nimua nodded her head in agreement and waded toward Iviana. "I knew you'd like it," she said.

"It's magical," Iviana insisted.

Nimua rolled her eyes, but smiled. "Lets get her out of here!"

ॐ13७

IVIANA AND NIMUA bid the Swimmers farewell and headed toward the area where the island homes were located when a little girl ran up to them, informing that Rhimesh wished for them to join her in her home as soon as they were able.

They promptly arrived and were surprised to find Darist there.

"I've been speaking with Darist, asking how he feels about your presence on the island so far." Rhimesh, sitting in a large comfortable looking chair, directed this statement to Iviana as though it were the simplest thing in the world. "I asked him because I know he is acquainted with you, but isn't, perhaps, so attached as Nimua, here."

Nimua and Iviana looked at Darist.

"What?" he asked. "It's not as if I told her to send Ivi home."

"No, he didn't," Rhimesh agreed. "On the contrary. He assures me your intentions are honest, even that you are interested in learning about our history."

Iviana peered up at Darist, confused by this last statement.

"You wanted to hear about the Age of the Great One..." he urged.

"Yes!" she said quickly. "I did."

"Well then, why not begin now." Rhimesh smiled. "I suppose the more you learn of us, the better we may know you, in time. Let us see, now... my, it was a glorious age, but it ended tragically, I'm afraid."

"What caused its end?" Iviana asked.

"A woman named Aradia. She'd fallen in love with an attached man and her love was not received by him. She was a bitter woman, for more than her spurned love, but in her bitterness, she tried to do away with the man who'd rejected her, our Realm Leader at the time and the great Tragor's favorite companion, Latos."

Iviana flinched at the name Latos, and her stomach grew ill when Aradia was named, but she couldn't conceive why.

"She did not succeed and, in a fury, Latos flew

her into your world, banishing her from ours. That was when we knew very little about your homeland. While there, she consorted with demonic forces and learned the dark arts of your world. It is written that, one night, she created a blazing, spell-bound fire to lure the dragons to her."

"Dragons are rather attracted to hot places," Darist interrupted.

"Yes," Rhimesh continued. "Not every dragon answered the fire's call, but a great many were baited. It was there, while gazing into the dark forces the fire was created with, her daemons possessed the dragons and filled their hearts with black fire."

"But why?" Iviana wanted to know.

"Dragons are generally gentle creatures... but they are also very powerful. Aradia wanted to control them, to use them to take over the Greater Archipelagos and ultimately have her revenge on those she felt had never understood her. She did not possess a Great Gift, you see, and this frustrated her, sending her down a dark path. But once the daemons had power over more than half of dragon-kind, they no longer needed her and she lost control of the dark dragons.

"I'm sure you've heard what they did to your royal fortress, Iviana, so many years ago, and to all those people in your towns and villages. The army of dark dragons rampaged your world before it could comprehend what was happening. Eventually, these dragons began to flood into our world. We fought them and were able to hold them off, but when Latos discovered who had created them and what was occurring in your land, he became angry with himself. He and Tragor gathered forces and led the battle against the great evil and, after a long, heartbreaking war, the dark dragons' numbers diminished. That kind of dragon is a rarity now, especially since your dragon slayers have taken the responsibility of destroying them upon themselves. Though how they could consider themselves true heroes is really beyond me," she added.

Iviana was surprised at her comment. "Why do you say that?" she asked.

"Latos and Tragor: they were always a duo to be reckoned with, but these battles revealed just how powerful they were together. They were thought to be unbeatable..." Rhimesh sighed. "But when they hunted Aradia down, she was able to succeed in what she'd originally attempted. She bested Latos. Regrettably, we may never be certain how it happened, but when you lose a Realm Leader of the Greater Archipelagos, all of its people feel it physically and we surely did."

Rhimesh finished and the three remained quiet for a long while.

Iviana had several questions, but one burned within her that she knew she must seek first. "Why is the time before all of that called the Age of the Great One?"

"A good question," Rhimesh said, "and an important one if you truly want to know our history and understand much of what we are today. Latos was Realm Leader of the Greater Archipelagos for only eighty years, but he was a Seer—one of those blessed with the capability of seeing what the Great One wishes to reveal—and his sight was the strongest we have ever known. It was said that Latos considered himself a friend of the Great One and it was with the wisdom he gained from his Friend that the Greater Archipelagos were able to gain the order and peace, the resplendent abundance that our realm has today. I am certain we would have come much further if the man were to have lived longer."

"Who became Realm Leader after Latos?" Iviana questioned.

"It was myself," Rhimesh answered, almost tiredly. Iviana's shock at this was so evident that the woman felt it necessary to explain. "At the time a person is appointed Realm Leader, that is when their aging process halts." She let out a long breath. "I have done the best I can, over these last, oh, hundred years or so, to keep the Greater Archipelagos as close as possible to the ideals that Latos established for us, but I am no Seer. It has been a difficult path."

"Rhimesh," Iviana began, finding it hard to breathe as she formed her next question. "This Latos... is it possible I'm related to him?"

Rhimesh hesitated and eyed her fiercely. "You've guessed accurately," she said. "Though, how you did, I cannot imagine." She raised an eyebrow, casting a curious glance on the young woman. "Yes, we believe you are his great-granddaughter."

Chills crept up Iviana's spine. If the information she received in her dream had been correct, would anything else from the dream haunt her waking life? She gulped. "How do you know?"

"That is another long story, Iviana, but I will try to condense it as it is nearly time for the evening supper. For one, you are the very image of the woman Latos' grandson married, but also because of that woman's connection to Naphtali."

Iviana couldn't believe the woman thought that was a valid explanation. "How were they connected?" she asked hungrily.

Rhimesh looked her over and forfeited. "I suppose I should begin by telling you of your grandfather, the youngest son of Latos and your father's father. His name was Damask. He loved his father, Latos, a great deal for they were very close while he lived. When Latos passed, your grandfather grew very angry with the Great One for allowing his father's death and he rejected the Great Gift he'd received from Him. Damask was what we call a Seeker and when the time came for the new Realm Leader to be selected, he refused to do his duty as Seeker. He would not follow the Great One's guidance to help find who would succeed Latos as our Realm Leader. Your father was one of two Seekers at the time. The other had passed in the Great War with the dark dragons, leaving your grandfather with the only gift of the Seeker in all the realm.

"This did not create an impossible situation, as there were other gifts such as seeing, but it is customary that a Seeker's gift be used for the task of discovering the appointed successor, according to the word of the Great One. Also, it is terribly difficult for a Seer to locate a single face in the midst of thousands of others over the whole of the Greater Archipelagos.

"At any rate, the islands were outraged at your grandfather's disrespect. They felt he'd turned his back on his people and I suppose he had, in a way. They were threatening to banish he and your grandmother, Lana, if he did not return to the Great One... and Damask told them they were free to do so. I suppose we should have known what would happen then. Maybe we did. The morning after the council had made their threats, your grandparents were nowhere to be found. It was assumed they had left through the door into Jaela's Cavern.

"It must have been close to sixty years later when a strange man by the name of Redden came through that door from your world, claiming he was the son of your grandfather, who had opened the door for him to enter. He said his father wished him to claim his birthright: the spot of land that Damask had lived in before he left for your world. I'm afraid the man was rather... presumptuous and left a sour taste in the mouths of the council. However, he was eventually allowed to reclaim the land and the house that stood on it.

"Some time later, it was discovered he had been wooing a daughter of one of the Island Leaders. Her name was Tasia. This was not necessarily a negative issue. It was only that Tasia was a good deal younger than Redden and her father did not approve of Redden at all. In fact, he had been one of those that opposed Redden repossessing his father's land."

"Redden was my father, then?" Iviana interrupted.

Rhimesh nodded meaningfully and continued. "One day, news broke out that Redden was to be married to the girl, but her father refused to give his blessing. The council asked that Redden and Tasia postpone their marriage until the conflict between Tasia's fiance and her father could come to some sort of resolve. They agreed and waited one year. When no good came of the delay, Tasia was discovered to have been gone from her father's home and neither her nor Redden could be found. It was eventually discovered they had escaped into Jaela's Cavern, like Redden's parents before him."

Iviana sat back in the chair she had taken when they entered Rhimesh's home and stared at the ceiling, trying to swallow back tears she did not understand. This did, at least, explain why those in the council considered her untrustworthy, but she still couldn't comprehend what her Naphtali had to do with it. "What of Naphtali?" she whispered.

"Ah, yes. After Tasia's mother had passed when she was very young, Naphtali became like a mother to the girl and helped in the raising of her. When your mother left, Naphtali was brokenhearted and blamed herself. She pleaded with the council to allow her to go and search for your mother in your realm, that she might convince them to return. They refused her and they deemed that if she chose to disobey their order, she would not be welcomed within the Greater Archipelagos again."

Iviana grew angry, trying to imagine anyone attempting to demand something of her beloved Naphtali. A thought occurred to her. "You would have been apart of the council at the time..." she almost dared Rhimesh.

Rhimesh nodded, "Yes, and I was not in agreement with the decision, but I was quite outnumbered."

Iviana sat up in her squeaky chair and declared, "But you're Realm Leader of all the Greater Archipelagos! You couldn't have overridden them?"

"That is not what a leader does, Iviana," the ageless woman replied. "I do not know how you came to be raised by the Healer, Naphtali, but be grateful, at least, that she chose her own path."

Iviana was still angry, but she couldn't help agreeing with Rhimesh. "I am."

"Then you are wiser than I assumed at first,"

Rhimesh spoke quietly, almost proudly, then put on her stern face again. "Now, it is time you all headed to the Grand Pavilion for the banquet."

ॐ

Nimua rushed Iviana to her temporary dwelling. When they reached it, Nimua insisted she choose Iviana's clothes for her and took great pains with Iviana's appearance, though Iviana couldn't imagine why.

"Alright, you are a vision," Nimua stated when she was done with her. Iviana tried to turn and look at herself in the mirror, but Nimua took her by the arm and declared, "No time! We've got to get to the banquet hall."

Iviana discovered the night before that the islands held banquets every night "but last night was in *your* honor," Nimua had insisted. *Sure,* Iviana had thought doubtfully. She knew the only one who wished to celebrate her presence on the island was Nimua.

"There you are," Darist said when the girls arrived in the Grand Pavilion. He quickly scooted a girl over who'd been flirting with him to make room for them. "You're late." He made a tisking motion at Nimua.

"We're sorry," Nimua answered sarcastically. "We didn't have your gifted strength to carry us here in a timely manner."

Darist rolled his eyes. Then he looked behind Iviana and said, "Oh, look who comes this way," and winked at Iviana before she could turn to see who it was.

"Hello," Nico said as he sat beside Iviana. "You ladies are late."

"We *know*, " Nimua assured him as she stole a glass of deep purple juice from a tray. Nico snatched two glasses.

"For you," he said, offering one of them to Iviana.

Iviana gave him a confused look, but accepted it, if awkwardly.

After an uncomfortable silence amidst the group, Nimua broke it with, "Iviana, have you ever enjoyed mango?"

"I don't think so," Iviana answered. "What's it like?"

"I'll get you some!" Nico declared and jumped to his feet to chase after a tray across the banquet hall.

Darist gave Nimua a quizzical look to which

Nimua responded with an unquenchable giggle.

"What?" Iviana asked.

"Nothing!" Nimua replied a little too loudly.

"Only that all Nico was able to talk about before you got here was how impatient he was for you to get here," Darist quickly informed Iviana before Nimua could get her elbow in his ribcage.

Iviana blinked. "Why?"

Darist raised an eyebrow. "I can only guess that the matchmaker is at work again."

"I am not!" Nimua defended.

"Ooh, no." Iviana's face turned red. "Please tell me you didn't." She cast a pitiful face at her friend.

It was apparent Nimua felt some regret over her actions, but she replied, "Oh, don't look so upset. I may have said a few things to encourage him in your direction, but it wasn't difficult to get him there. He was already interested."

"And the matchmaker can't help herself, " Darist added.

"It's for her own good. She was so terrified at the thought of me finding her a man that I knew I had to. She needs to know your kind isn't scary," Nimua responded, poking Darist on the nose.

"I'm not afraid of men, Nimua. I just... don't want the attention."

"How couldn't you?" Nimua asked, almost shocked. "You just don't know how fun it is."

"For Nimua," Darist added again.

"Stop acting like you know me *sooo* well, Darist," Nimua said.

"He sort of does, though," Nico put in as he sat down next to Iviana with the mango. "Here you are." He handed her the plate.

"Thanks," Iviana answered.

The rest of the banquet continued without much exchange between Iviana and Nico. Brenna, the beautiful Swimmer from that morning, and a girl named Leilyn eventually came to join them, the latter attempting to drape herself around Darist who rolled his eyes and scooted a little closer to Nimua.

Iviana discovered she very much liked Brenna, who had an adventurous disposition and was very in-tune with nature. She spent her life researching and cultivating it and was fascinated by everything Iviana shared about Kierlia's environment. It pleased Iviana to speak about her homeland with someone who was so interested.

Leilyn was another story, however, for she refused to give Iviana any attention whatever, even when Iviana had spoken directly to her. It was as if she thought Iviana too far beneath her interest to be treated as any human ought. This was discomfiting, but Iviana concentrated on the friend she was making in Brenna.

Finally, the banquet came to a close and the islanders left in groups until the six young people were the only ones remaining in the hall.

"I suppose we all ought to be getting home," Nico said regretfully to Iviana. "They don't like us out too late."

"I think Ivi broke that rule last night, though," Darist tattled. "How'd you pull it off?" he asked her.

"I wasn't out that late," she defended.

"You shouldn't do that," Nico insisted. "It could be dangerous. In fact, I think I ought to escort-"

"Yes, why don't I escort you home tonight, Ivi," Darist interrupted before Nico had a chance to finish. "Come along, ol' gal," Darist said as he stood and offered Iviana his arm, "Good night, Nico... Nimua, Brenna, Leilyn.

Iviana noted the icy glare Leilyn gave her, the first sign of acknowledgment since they'd met, and cast a nod to pitiful Nico when he told her he would see her later.

When the two were out of hearing distance from the group, Darist turned to her and said, "I hope you don't mind, but when I realized what Nico was about to gallantly offer–"

"Thank you," Iviana interrupted. "Though I'm sure you'd have rather escorted Nimua." Her eyes sparkled innocently, if not mischievously.

Darist blinked, asking, "Is it really that obvious? You haven't even been here very long."

"It is—at least to me."

He was quiet a moment before saying, "I think she pretends she doesn't care for me."

Iviana looked up at him. "Pretends?"

He smiled. "I hope so, anyway. I think I've cared for her since we were children, but lately she's been distant." He looked her in the eyes as they walked. "I know you haven't been here long, but do you have any idea why she would do that?"

"No," she answered, then added hesitantly, "Perhaps she wants to keep her options open. Perhaps she's afraid of being trapped on the island forever if she ties herself down."

"Has she said anything like that?"

"No, I only wonder."

"You won't say anything about my feelings for her will you?"

"Of course not."

"Thank you," he replied, then chuckled when they arrived at the little path leading to her home "Enjoy avoiding Nico tomorrow."

❧14☙

THE NEXT DAY, Iviana awoke feeling restless. She had not had much time alone since she'd been on the island and, though grateful for that, she wanted to do a little exploring on her own. So, quickly dressing herself, she headed out the patio door, stealing fruit from a nearby tree.

It was a beautiful morning. Iviana enjoyed the warm, tropical breezes blowing gently over her face and hair. She had always hated the cold and detested the crisp winters in Kierelia. Here, there was no winter, so she was told, and Iviana thought she would remain in this world forever, if only for that reason.

She came upon a row of tall bushes covered in berries and began to stroll beside them, enjoying their fruit as she went.

"Kurnin, you're not being fair," a voice said from

behind one of the fruity hedges.

Iviana thought the voice belonged to Rhimesh and guessed this was where her home was located. She did not at all intend to stay and eavesdrop; she only wished to go on her way, but what she heard next stopped her cold.

"That dragon girl is a poison to our island, just like her father," she heard Kurnin, the Island Leader, say. "We allowed him to live freely among us and, well, you're aware of what took place. You, more than anyone, know what a poor decision that was, considering, if I remember correctly, it was highly influenced by your words to the council at the time."

"You were yet very young at the time, Kurnin, and I believe your memory of the matter isn't something to be relied on," Rhimesh answered tiredly.

"I remember enough. Therefore, I know what this girl is akin to. After all, we really know nothing about her. She could be seducing our young men for all we know, like her father did her mother. She's influencing our *children*, Rhimesh. We've all seen the way Naii's daughter worships her. Who's to say the rest won't follow? And what are they following? The offspring of one of the Greater Archipelagos' greatest mistakes."

"Kurnin," Rhimesh spoke soundly, silencing the leader for the moment, at least. "You forget she is also the great-granddaughter of Latos. And, if you'll permit, I would like to mention that I have never believed the rumors spread about her father. His care for the girl was true, whether or not his every action was correct. And yet, you are correct. Correct in that we do not know much about her, and certainly we do not know that she is a seducer, or a bad influence. I, for one, have viewed nothing at all of the sort."

"I *have*, I'm afraid, seen things I wish I had not," Kurnin responded with artificial concern.

There was silence on that side of the hedge for a time until Rhimesh said slowly, "What is it you *claim* to have seen, Kurnin?"

Kurnin cleared his throat before saying curtly, "I do not think it wise to repeat."

There was silence again, larger than the last. And then: "Likely," Rhimesh replied icily.

"I will say this, however," he began again, sounding as though he wished he could backtrack, but knowing he had no choice but to move forward, "she may be related to Latos, but I think she could very well undo everything Latos did for this great world. After all, she has already broken laws, such as entering our realm without express permission from our council. That is just one more attribute she shares with her father."

His every word hit like physical punches at Iviana's heart. Everything he said exuded a putrid spirit, almost as though not all of his words were his own—could not possibly be. They were too hateful to be coming from the mouth of the Island Leader, whom she had never even spoken with directly. Her head ached and she began to feel dizzy; she wanted to defend herself or scream at him, but she couldn't. She could not move. Even breathing was a struggle.

The first dark clouds she had seen since coming to this world began to curl in overhead and she felt as though the whole darkened sky was going to cave in on her small frame.

Meanwhile, Kurnin continued, "What I mean to say is, these people turn up out of nowhere and we are expected to openly accept them into our society? I believe it is offensive and disrespectful to the Great One."

When Rhimesh was too dumbstruck to respond, the man took it as encouragement and continued, "After all, Rhimesh, she is only a little girl. We can easily be rid of her, for the sake of our children and the Great One."

Iviana would have heard him sigh in self-righteous exhaustion, but suddenly a gasp sounded behind her, causing her to cry out in surprise before turning around to find that Nimua's mother had been standing there, gazing at her with teary eyes. Iviana didn't know how long she'd been watching her eavesdrop. She clamped her hands over her mouth after the frightened yelp escaped her, but when she turned back to look behind the bushes, she found the eyes of Rhimesh and Kurnin on her.

The next thing she knew, she was running, ignoring Naii's compassionate voice calling for her to wait, and she ran faster than she ever remembered running in her life. It was as though the wind were sweeping beneath her feet and helping her float across the landscape; as if she were in a dream and she could fly. But she couldn't, and so she continued running, not caring what Naii or anyone thought of her.

Nevertheless, she did feel sorry that she ran from Naii and hoped the kind woman wasn't trying to catch up to her. After all, Naii hadn't been the one to say those hurtful things; she had only startled Iviana and made her give up her hiding place behind the hedge.

Her lungs began to ache after a while and the cold wind whispered stinging insults against her ears.

She wanted to stop, but her eyes were leaking, her face was a mess with tears and heartache and people were staring at her as she went. If she stopped, they would ask what ailed her, or worse yet, they would only stare and wonder what state of mind she was in. So she went, feeling as though the trees around her pointed the way for her, and yet they mocked her, for they were leading her to a place where she would be alone. Still she followed where they led until she had almost reached her hut, but just as she came to the lane, she defied it and the trees and ran for the valley where the dragons dwelt.

It wasn't until her dragon's startled form was before her that she stopped—stopped everything—running, crying, breathing.

She stood there a while, staring into his eyes, his eyes gazing back with more concern than she thought a dragon could show or feel, and then she threw her arms around him and sobbed into his shoulder with his head nuzzled against her, comforting her.

She had thought to go back to her world, if Tragor was willing to take her, but she knew if she did, it meant never seeing her friends again and that included Tragor. He could not live with her near the village, even if he wanted to, or he would eventually be discovered and slain.

Quiet with numbness, she eventually gained control of herself and turned from Tragor with a longing pat to walk herself home. Once within, she melted into a kitchen chair and began to sob the sobs of someone who longs for *love* and is not receiving what her heart so desperately desires.

It was some time before she was startled by a hand placed on her shoulder and Naii's voice whispering, "Don't fret, my dear." And then the woman's hand began gently soothing Iviana's back and, when Iviana did not tell her to go, the woman knelt on the ground and put her arms around the girl and there she held her and whispered comfort. "It's alright, sweet. I've got you," she said. "This will all pass, I promise."

৪০

A while later, the sound of boiling water sounded through the kitchen while Iviana sat upon her chair, wrapped generously in a large white blanket.

"There we are," Naii said after pouring the hot water into a pitcher of cured tea leaves. She then reached into a cupboard and procured a couple of vessels to pour the refreshment into.

"I didn't even know those were up there," Iviana commented with a little humor.

"Oh, I suppose we should show you around the kitchen at some point. I imagine we do things a little differently than those in your world. I hope you're being fed enough."

Iviana accepted the mug offered her and stole a sip of the tea, letting its healing power rejuvenate her body. "Oh, yes, very well. I don't believe I've ever eaten quite so healthily in my life."

Each morning a new basket of various foods was found in her little kitchen and, though it often contained breads and cheeses, she was provided with almost an overabundance of fruits and vegetables.

Naii sat upon another of the kitchen chairs and enjoyed the cup she had poured for herself and Iviana stole the moment to speak what was on her mind. "I'm wondering if it would be wise for me to return to my home world."

Naii pondered this a time before answering, "Kurnin is a problem and has always been so, but more so, I think, as he has grown older. He is an embittered man. Rhimesh and I have been wondering what should be done with him. After all, we are the capital island of the Greater Archipelagos and our leadership should reflect that."

"Surely, most islanders respect his opinion, though, as he is leader of the island?"

"Yes," Naii replied. "Unfortunately he has many loyal followers."

Iviana sighed and said, "I'm afraid my staying will create... issues... for you all and, honestly, I don't know that I have much of a desire to remain here any longer."

Naii nodded. "That is more than understandable after what you've just heard, but I think—" she hesitated. "I think you would prevail if you remained here and I believe... that it is what my mother, Naphtali, would have hoped for. She did love her home here and I can only imagine she would wish for you to come to love it as well."

Iviana hesitated as well. "Naii, can I ask you something?"

"Of course."

"How old were you when Naphtali followed my parents into Kaern against the wishes of the council?"

"I was about your age," the woman answered.

Iviana nodded.

Guessing Iviana's thoughts, Naii continued, "But I was married at the time and so, when my mother told me she was going, yes, I was broken, but I knew I was not alone and so did she. When she left... it was because she knew she had to, as though the Great One was asking her to and her heart would break if she didn't. I now wonder that her purpose was to take care of you, when you came along."

Iviana was startled by the idea. "The Great One? Why would He do something like that for me? Before I was even born? He couldn't have known about me yet."

"The Great One knows many things that we do not understand. And I believe He takes care of each of us, often when we haven't any idea that He is doing so."

Though such an idea warmed Iviana, she did not truly understand it. She hoped she would someday.

"I think I might stay... at least for a little while," Iviana admitted hesitantly.

Naii smiled. "Good," she said. Then added, "I'm afraid it's getting late and... there are some matters with the council that I would like to take care of. Will you be alright?"

"Yes," Iviana answered with a smile. "Thank you, Naii."

"Any time." Naii hugged her. "By the way, I believe Nimua and Darist are down at Swimmer's

Point. Just thought you'd like to meet them there before the banquet begins."

∞

"Ivi, we haven't seen you all day!" Nimua exclaimed as Iviana joined them on the beach. "Where have you been?"

"Found out I'm a menace to the realm," Iviana answered.

"No kidding?" Darist asked sarcastically.

"Mhm," she answered and nodded proudly. "That much hasn't changed, anyway."

"Of course," Nimua added wryly. "That's why we're friends with you."

"Fantastic. Looking forward to influencing you for the worse. Maybe I could instruct you both in the art of sorcery." Iviana flashed them a dry smile.

"That'd be great," Darist put in. "One of us could pull an Aradia."

They laughed, but the conversation seemed to have gone too far by that point, so they settled themselves.

"Seriously though, what are you talking about?" Nimua asked her.

Iviana smiled. "Nothing. What have you two been up to?"

Nimua answered, "Darist was asked to pull a huge tree out of Brenna's garden and he did it. Then hauled it off to be made into firewood on top of that. He's not usually given the chance to do anything quite so... ostentatious."

Darist smirked. "Of course I have. You just don't know about it."

"Oh, right, like I don't know *everything* you do on this little island."

"*Alright...* you two," Iviana jumped in before the bickering entirely stole the conversation. Turning to Darist, she continued, "That's incredible. Why wasn't I invited to view the spectacle?"

"Oh, you would've been," Nimua answered her. "Nico went by your hut to invite you, but you weren't home, so we all went to see if you were in the dragon's lair, but Tragor was lazily grazing without his new favorite. It was then that we quite gave up on you."

Iviana made a noise of disappointment. "I wish I had been there. I've never actually seen Darist's gift in action.

Darist jumped to his feet in earnest. "I'll show you something now."

"Like what?" Iviana asked.

"Like..." he scanned the area with his eyes. "Um..."

"You sure the gift really exists?" Iviana teased.

Nimua laughed. "Haha, you caught us. We sure fooled you, didn't we?"

Darist had a look of enlightenment. "Wait here," he said.

Nimua chortled again. "We should ditch him and go for a swim."

Iviana laughed with her, but disagreed. "I really want to see this; whatever it ends up being."

Darist returned with chairs in hand.

"That's... pretty impressive," Iviana commented.

He smirked. "Sit down." He gestured to the chairs. "You too, Nimua."

"Oh, no, not me," Nimua fussed.

"Ah, come on, Nim," he begged with dreamy eyes.

"Fine," she answered dryly.

Iviana obeyed too and, next thing she knew, she was no longer looking levelly at the shoreline before her, but down upon it. She gave a little squeal of excitement above the left side of Darist's shoulder.

Nimua replied from his right, "*Please*, don't encourage him. His ego's been fluffed enough for one day." She turned to Darist and said, "Put us down."

Darist did so and, once on the ground, Iviana admitted, "I might not be a tree, but that was fairly amazing."

Darist stood before the ladies and bowed. Nimua's response was to toss sand at his face and Iviana jumped between the two before they could bury one another.

৪ 15 ৫

THE NEXT FEW months passed more quickly than Iviana could have imagined. In the early mornings, she grew to anticipate the damp, sun-warmed air that arose all around her like a misty blanket of magic come to welcome another fair day. The rest of her day was often spent exploring.

It was Brenna, the Swimmer, who introduced her to a part of the island with colorful, dense foliage and bright green trees making up a brilliant tropical forest. Iviana had been afraid they would find themselves lost once within, but Brenna assured her the area wasn't large enough for them to be lost for more than a day.

At one point, while they hiked through the island forest, they passed a large, dark-gray rock that Brenna introduced as "Old Rock Face" because it roughly resembled the face of an old man. It was as they slowed at this point that Iviana's leg lightly brushed against a plant with slender brown branches sporting little green leaves and peculiar pink buds. The moment her leg grazed it, a small movement caught her eye causing Iviana to look back at it and bend down to take a closer look. The little buds of the plant had tiny whimsical balls at the end of numerous ultra-thin pink petals that stuck out sporadically. Iviana bent nearer and lightly poked a section of the leaves.

Immediately they folded and weaved themselves up from her touch as though it were alive. She tried again and it shielded itself from her as it had before. Iviana turned to Brenna for an explanation. She informed Iviana that it was called a "touch-me-not", or mimosa pudica, and it was gravely shy of touch. But she assured Iviana that the leaves would open up again in a few minutes, so they waited until, at last, Brenna's information proved correct.

This occasion only intensified the mystery the island held for Iviana, inspiring her to explore until there was no more to be seen.

On her journeys across the island, Iviana often traveled alone so she could linger in certain places, undisturbed by others wanting to move faster. She longed to study all she could about life in this place.

Sometimes Iviana would find a plant or animal that so intrigued her, she would have to observe it and take notes in a little diary. During one such outing, she discovered that when she touched various plants and herbs, she could feel healing power pumping within them. At first she wondered if she were only imagining it, but when she exchanged notes with the island Healer, he informed her this was a part of the Gift of the Healer. He also told her, her Gift for finding curative species was far sharper than any he had ever encountered.

On another occasion, she resolved to follow a crystal-clear river, wishing to discover where its source lay. This occupied almost an entire day, for it mazed every which way.

After some time, she came to a point in the river where it became a small stream and she supposed she must be very close to the end. It continued, however, and so she did as well, moving as the water rose slightly higher in altitude amidst the tropical forest until the little stream grew wider once again.

Finally, she discovered a rushing, roaring dissonance that sounded like rumbling thunder. It emanated from the grandest waterfall Iviana had ever seen (and she had seen many while following the river). The water plunged from hundreds of feet above into a large, clear pool, cascading water and mist into the pool. Peering closer, Iviana could just spot a cave behind the fall and so leaped into the deep water and down low beneath the waterfall so as not to be beaten by its force. She swam until she arose again behind it.

The cave was the same gray rock found all throughout the island and it was mostly dark within except for a hole at the side of its roof that sprayed in beams of golden, shimmering sunlight mixed with splashes of sparkling water. She tried to reach out and touch the sunlight as though it were a tangible thing, but found it was like any other ray of light. Her eyes followed where the ray pointed and her attention was caught by a light shimmer along the floor and walls of the cave rock. She touched the golden glitter in the rock and decided it was either magic or gold. Whichever it was, Iviana had never been so near to either.

She laid back in the pool and sighed, breathing in the fragrance of the honey-scented water and realized she did not care to reach the source of the river any longer. Rather, she enjoyed her own secret place and found serenity in it.

The next day, however, after hearing of Iviana's venture, Nimua decided they would go as a group to discover the stream's source.

"But I told you I don't care to know it," Iviana told her. "It took me the whole day just to get as far as I did."

"Well, today you will have friends to push you along. You know you only took so long because you like to dawdle. But today is not a day for dawdling; it is a day for exploration... and discovery!" Nimua answered her enthusiastically as she bounced out the door to go and inform Darist of their plans for the day.

Iviana sighed and could not help the smile that crept over her face. She followed Nimua out the door.

"We're doing what?" Darist asked when the young women arrived at his home.

"Finding a source," Nimua replied shortly, insinuating that he should have understood her the first time she explained.

He thought a moment, then answered, "Alright... I'm in." He turned to Iviana as Nimua began leading them down the path. "Source of what?" he asked her.

She smiled. "A river."

He raised his brows and shrugged. "Fun."

When they found Brenna at Swimmer's Point,

Nimua asked that she join them as she knew the forest better than anyone and would keep them from getting hurt or lost. Nimua was not well acquainted with nature and was taking no chances. The party grew, however, when, at sight of Darist, Leilyn invited herself along, as did Nico, to Iviana's secret dismay.

Even so, it was Nico who caught Iviana when she slid on a slippery patch of earth and began to fall backward. Indeed, from the moment Nico had been invited on their quest, he had not left Iviana's side.

He had been content to remain quiet in the beginning of the hike, but once they had traveled a while, he became bubbly and talkative with Iviana. This wouldn't have been so bad if she were able to keep up with the rest of the hikers, but Nico's conversation kept demanding her attention and, somehow, they kept falling behind the others as she endeavored to listen. She wondered if he were setting their pace behind the others on purpose.

When Nico caught her after her slip, he did not immediately let her go, insisting he would help steady her again, but she was quite certain that she was balanced enough and told him so. Finally he forced her to sit upon the ground so he could examine her ankle to be sure she had not hurt it.

"Nico, I'm *fine*," she told him sourly, wishing the others would slow down for them.

"You could injure your ankle more if you continue to walk on it after a twist," he told her patiently, trying to get a hold of the foot that kept evading him.

"I can assure you it's not twisted; I would know."

"Just sit still," he responded after he had a hold of the foot. He tossed her his charming half smile and examined it.

Iviana wanted to scream in frustration until she heard footsteps behind her. Nico quickly stood to his feet.

"What's up, Darist?" he said in a funny tone. "I was just making sure Ivi wasn't wounded after she slipped."

Darist came around and looked at Iviana's intact ankles. "Here, lets check them," he said in a helpful tone with a hidden touch of sarcasm, and assisted Iviana to her feet. "Can you stand?" he asked her.

Iviana smiled. "Mhm."

"Good." Darist smiled back. "I think I'll hang out back here with you two and see if I can't get you caught up with the rest of us."

"Oh, we're just fine, Darist," Nico insisted. "Ivi

has me to help her."

Iviana choked and Darist patted her on the back, saying, "It's alright, Ivi. Nico and I will help you along."

Iviana swatted Darist's arm off her back while she finished choking. Darist didn't quite suppress a chuckle.

"Alright, then," Nico said," but I'll take her pack for her."

"That sure is kind of you," Darist replied, taking the pack off Iviana's back and tossing it at him.

It wasn't long before the three caught up to where the others had decided to wait for them.

"What has kept you all?" Nimua asked with a smirk. "We've been waiting all day."

"Right, since the sun hasn't even risen above the treetops yet," Iviana answered blithely.

"Besides," Darist added with a smirk, "Ivi tripped and Nico had to help her get on her feet again."

Nimua pasted a smile on her lips, but glared at Darist. "Then maybe you should have left him to it," she said.

Iviana heard Darist whisper in Nimua's ear, "Ivi doesn't like him and you know how forward he can be."

She heard Nimua whisper back, "Maybe she *will*

like him if you leave it alone."

When they started again, Iviana was glad to find that Darist didn't heed Nimua's words and remained at her side so long as Nico did.

As Nico often required her attention on him and him alone, they still were not quite able to keep time with the others. However, they did not fall as far behind as they had before. Darist's helpful comments assisted in this. "Would you like me to take your packs for a while?" he would say. "Your pace is getting a little tired." Nico would then pick up his pace and say that he simply did not want to tire Iviana.

Iviana shut up her mouth.

At noontime, they stopped for lunch. Iviana was happy to be among women once again. Things at the end of the party were getting a little tense.

"We've almost reached the waterfall I told you about," Iviana commented when they were sitting restfully together, enjoying the food that Brenna had prepared for them.

"Good!" Nimua huffed. "This is more tiring than I thought it would be."

Brenna laughed and reminded, "This was your idea, you know."

"Right," Nimua agreed. "And I'm not saying it

was a bad idea either—just... phew." She rubbed her face. "I'm tired."

"Thank goodness for this breeze," Iviana said as another gust of wind blew through her curly hair.

"Here's my question," Nico began. "How can the source of this river be coming from up the mountain? It's not as though we have any snow-capped peaks or anything."

"That's why we're doing this!" Nimua said excitedly. "It's an adventure and who knows what we'll find in the end."

Brenna giggled. "It's a river's source. It's not going to be that exciting," she said.

"The waterfall is beautiful, though, even if the source isn't," Iviana said.

Brenna nodded. "I think I may have been there before—to the waterfall, I mean. It's brilliant."

"It is," Iviana agreed. "Did you see the cave?"

"Cave?" Brenna shrugged. "I guess I missed that. I haven't hiked up that far for a few years."

"Well, I, for one, am looking forward to whatever we find," Darist said cheerily. "I haven't been on a lengthy hike in a long time."

"How do you stay in such great shape, Darist?" Leilyn asked, casting him a brilliant smile.

"Well," he began, "it doesn't take much. Strength

is my gift. I hate to admit it, but I really don't have to work too hard at it."

"I work out on a daily basis," Nico put in. "Swimming is actually a pretty good workout."

"Oh, it shows," Leilyn answered. "Too bad Iviana isn't as diligent in her daily regime or she would be able to keep up with the rest of us. We could actually be there by now."

Iviana choked for the second time that day. Everyone else was quiet.

"I think," began Darist, "we'd all be surprised at Ivi's pace if, perhaps, there were fewer of us in the group."

Iviana sent Darist a small smile and hoped Nico did not pick up on what he was implying. She did not enjoy Nico's attention, but she didn't want his feelings hurt either. She looked to where he sat and saw that he was contentedly enjoying the mango in his hand.

Leilyn, however, cast Iviana a solid, icy glare. Iviana noticed this, but hoped and nearly assumed she'd misread her. She did not need enemies.

Brenna stood to her feet. "I think that's a long enough break," she said.

Iviana was less pleased that Nico had not understood Darist's earlier comment when he was by her side again and slowing her pace. Darist was with them as well, however, which made Iviana feel more comfortable.

After a few minutes, Iviana was pleased to find that Leilyn had, for whatever reason, hiked back to where they were and set her pace to theirs. The girl then jumped into lengthy conversation with Nico, awing over his Swimmer's speed and making remarks about his biceps. This altogether removed his attention from Iviana, making it possible for her and Darist to pick up their pace a bit.

Darist leaned near Iviana and commented, "Looks like you may not have to worry about undesired attention anymore."

Iviana smiled at the thought and looked back to where Leilyn was, grateful that she had joined them. However, after sending Iviana another very clear glare, Leilyn quickly jogged up to where Iviana and Darist were and began flirting with Darist.

Iviana glanced back at Nico who looked bewildered and disappointed. He did not speak again after that—not even to Iviana. Meanwhile, Leilyn wholly ignored Iviana and did not allow Darist time to include her in the conversation. This left Iviana alone and confused until they reached the waterfall.

"Ivi, it's beautiful!" Nimua exclaimed excitedly.

There it was again: the water falling harshly into the fevered body of water below. The deep, clear water of the pond still sparkled in the illumination of the sun and all about them was like the sound of fireworks.

"Where is the cave?" Brenna asked over the sound of the waterfall.

"We have to swim to it," Iviana yelled and pointed beneath the water.

"Is it safe?" Leilyn asked, peering at the place where the waterfall hit the water.

"It should be if we swim low enough," Iviana answered.

When Leilyn looked doubtful, Brenna offered to share her Swimmer's gift so that she could breathe through the swim.

"No, that's alright. I want Nico to take me," Leilyn answered and tossed Nico a grin.

Nico smiled back, but looked confused and said he thought he would take Iviana.

"That's alright," Iviana assured him. "I've done it before."

"Just accept his help and stop playing with his feelings," Leilyn suddenly snapped at her and jumped into the pool without warning. Brenna rushed in after her. Everyone else stood blinking at Iviana.

Iviana didn't understand what had happened. She was embarrassed and her instinct was to run back to her hut where she could be alone, but she also felt compelled to confront Leilyn. Moving fast before she lost her courage, she leaped into the water and dove deep beneath the cascading fall.

About to swim up into the cave, she noticed a struggle between Brenna and Leilyn within the water. When she swam closer, she saw that Leilyn's toga was caught by something and Brenna was trying to pull her free. Iviana was thankful she still practiced the habit of carrying a dagger in her belt and swam over to them. She quickly cut the end of the skirt and urged Brenna to help her pull the exhausted Leilyn out of the water.

"Let go of me!" Leilyn shouted when they were able to take in their first breaths of air behind the waterfall. She kicked away from Iviana and pulled herself onto a piece of rock.

"What's the matter with you?" Brenna asked Leilyn, astonished. "She just helped you!"

"Oh, she did no such thing! All she cares about is getting attention," Leilyn replied angrily. "Attention from *men*, that is."

Iviana swam to where she was on the rock and tried to speak, but Leilyn turned on her full force.

"I'm sick of watching you throw yourself at Nico and Darist. I don't know what girls are like in your world, but here, we don't steal other people's beaus and play with their heads."

"Leilyn..." Iviana hesitated. She didn't know where to begin. "I'm not trying to steal anyone's beau. I don't understand what I've done."

"Oh, of course. You're perfectly innocent. 'Darist, I need you to help me up the mountain,'" she said in a mocking voice. "'Oh, and Nico, will you carry my pack?' It's disgusting, Iviana! I mean, Nico is one thing, but do you have to steal Darist from me?"

Iviana stuttered, trying to think of something to say, some way of defending herself, but words would not form in her mouth. "Leilyn, I-" she tried.

"Save it, Iviana. You're just like your father and we all saw it coming. No one trusts you. And you should probably be aware that we see right through you. You don't belong here." Leilyn looked as though she would go on, but needed to catch her breath.

Their was an uncomfortable cough behind them and Iviana turned to find Nimua, Nico and Darist. Iviana was humiliated and thought she might dive beneath the water and not come up for a while.

What was worse was that no one said anything. It was as though a spell had been cast and everyone was speechless.

Finally, Brenna spoke, "We're all... tired. Maybe we should head back."

Nico agreed. Leilyn dove beneath the water in a huff. Nimua and Darist looked at each other. Then Nimua spoke to Brenna, "We'll leave in a bit. I think we'll just rest here for a while."

Brenna nodded, took a disappointed Nico by the arm and led him away.

It was quiet in the cave then and Iviana was trying not to lose it.

Nimua said quietly, "Come on. We're going to find the source."

ജ

The sun was just beginning to set when Iviana, Nimua and Darist had nearly reached the top of the mountain. All across the sky were pinks and oranges with hints of purple trying to splash themselves into the splendorous mix. Then, finally...

There it was.

The three were made speechless by what they

saw. They stared a while, exploring it with their eyes. There, at the very top of the mountain, was a small crater holding a gleaming pool of water. More interesting still was the beehive of a pinkish-gold hue shaped against a corner of the rock that made up the pool, surrounded by a few docile bees buzzing about. Honey flowed generously from their hive into the pool of water.

The water's intense blue swirled with a deep amber and shimmered in the rays of the sun, so still it had the appearance of smooth glass. Slowly, it flowed over the edge of the rock as though it were just full enough to offer what it contained with the mountainside. The atmosphere was thick as though a presence resided here and somehow the whole place was musical and ringing.

They bent near and looked for the bottom of the pool, but could not see it.

Iviana released a great sigh of relief and asked, "But where does the water come from?"

Nimua replied quietly and absently, almost whimsically, "Marquen says that, though we in the village do not see rainfall often, except during a certain season of time, it rains heavily and often over the rocky cliffs and mountains. That's why the early-morning fog is so thick at times. We don't always see the rain up where it's so high and in places where the forest and trees camouflage it. Often, it just appears as mist or fog; a blur in the distance, I suppose."

Iviana had a random desire, but wondered whether or not it was wrong to follow through. It was so quiet and lovely and perfect in this place and she did not want to force the peace out of it because of a self-indulgent whim. So, to quench her desire to slide into the quiescent water, slowly, she knelt down in her shorter white toga and lightly, almost gracefully, touched the surface of the pool with the very tip of her delicate middle finger, causing a small, willowy ripple to ring out from where she grazed it.

Then there were more rings and ripples and they were clashing with the ones she had made and she was in wonderment until she looked up and saw Nimua slowly placing one of her long, slender legs into the water and then the other until she fluidly pushed herself into the pool. Her movements looked like a dance making Iviana wonder if everything they did in this place was honeyed and lyrical.

Iviana didn't realize she was staring until a melodious giggle escaped from Nimua's mouth and she insisted to Iviana that wading within the water was not a crime as far as she knew. Iviana smiled, sat upon the rocky edge and dipped her legs in, resting back on her palms.

"I'm sure we're not the first to have found this place," Nimua commented, "but I've never heard mention of it."

"My great-grandmother used to say Latos spent a great deal of time in these mountains so that he could commune with the Great One," Darist offered, "and when he came down from the mountains, he smelled sweet as her honey rolls." He rolled up his pant legs and sat next to Iviana, dropping his bare feet into the water.

"I'm glad the others didn't come," Nimua said. Iviana and Darist agreed, but they did not say so—did not have to.

"I'm sorry for what Leilyn said," Darist spoke. "I didn't know she cared for me that way."

Iviana smiled, but wished he hadn't mentioned it. She didn't want anything to poison the atmosphere of this place. "Make no mention of it," she answered. "I shared friendship with no one before I came here, except Naphtali, and I'm just grateful for right now."

Darist looked her in the eyes as though reading how lonely and rejected she had felt all the years of her life and Nimua saw Darist see her and she wished she could see it too. She knew the two were kindred spirits from the start—they were so much alike—but she almost wished it weren't so. She couldn't help but want Iviana for herself. She, too, had been lonely at times, but it was a lonesomeness born of every day being the same and always wanting more out of life. She just knew there was more—that there must be more—and then there was Iviana and she hoped that Iviana held the key to freeing her from her suffocating cage.

Iviana felt him see her too and it made her feel vulnerable and so she dropped the rest of herself into the pool and was surprised to find that she could not feel its floor.

She bobbed her head back up from within the water and asked Nimua, "How deep do you think this is?"

Nimua smiled. "I don't know, but I'll bet it's pretty deep." Without a word of explanation, she dove head first into the pool and disappeared from sight.

"I wasn't expecting that," Iviana said hesitantly and a little laughingly.

Darist grinned. "She's always been like that: spontaneous, sometimes a little crazy. She makes everything fun, that's for sure."

After a few seconds passed, Iviana grew nervous

and asked, "Should I dive down after her?"

Darist shook his head. "No, it's too dark down there; you might collide with her." He added a little nervously, "She better come up soon, though..."

It wasn't too much longer before Nimua's golden head popped out again and she declared breathlessly, pushing her long hair out of her face, "Honestly, I think I'd rather not know how deep it is."

ಞ16ೲ

THAT NIGHT, Naii appeared at Iviana's door. She informed Iviana that Rhimesh had regarded her passion for the exploration of the island and now offered her a visit to another of the nearby islands: the Isle of Knowledge. Iviana was thrilled, not only because she had secretly been longing to view more of the realm, but she could not help hoping that it meant she had gained some portion of trust from the islanders. She had felt that, over the course of time she'd spent on the Isle of Dragons, the people were growing friendlier toward her and perhaps more accustomed to her presence among them.

The thought of getting away for a while after what had happened with Leilyn did not discredit the chance either. She hastily agreed.

The following morning, Iviana met Naii at the

shoreline where she'd spent some time on one of her first nights: the place she had seen the blue fish. She wondered if they were traveling to the island she had seen in the distance that evening.

It soon became apparent that they would be escorted by Swimmers to their destination. Though Iviana couldn't imagine how they would ever find the strength to make it all that way, she was intrigued by the idea.

Naii winked at her and asked, "You ready?"

Iviana grinned a little nervously and nodded.

She had had no need to worry over the trip, however. The Swimmers were anointed with great strength beneath the cover of water and Iviana and Naii did not have to move a muscle as they were pulled by the Swimmer's gift.

During the curious, underwater trip, Iviana began to worry that her first appearance on the new island would entail her skin being profusely prune-like and she hated the idea of looking like a fruit at her initial meeting with the people.

When at last they pulled up to the shore of the island, her first steps were extremely wet, but she was relieved to find that she did not look like a prune and assumed it must be part of the gift.

On the Isle of Knowledge, Iviana was warmly

received and welcomed by the inhabitants. It seemed their friendship with Naii was so substantial, it spilled onto Iviana as well (a reality she did not mind at all).

Immediately, she was surrounded with Teachers and Healers who wanted to trade what knowledge she had of her home realm for whatever knowledge they could share. It became evident that these people took learning and knowing very seriously just as respect of the dragons was essential on the Isle of Dragons.

It was only the second day of her arrival when Iviana was asked to speak before some of the islanders to share facts and stories about Kierelia. Iviana froze when asked, as she had recently learned she did not do well in front of crowds, but she was so honored and ready to speak about her own world with anyone who would listen that she consented.

The place the lecture was held seemed to be in the center of the busiest part of the island. There were colorful tents of blues, purples and reds and curtains and flowers hung all around her. The place was busy with gossip and laughing and the people were affectionate with one another—a far cry from the cold feeling Iviana often felt when on the capital island. A good number of the people had gathered before her and were ready for her to begin. Looking over the crowd, she thought she might run. Even so, surrounded with warm hearts and eager ears, Iviana gave her address.

It was after her speech to the islanders that Iviana met a woman who was very much unlike the people of the Isle of Knowledge. Indeed, she was different from anyone in the Greater Archipelagos, she was sure.

Iviana was surrounded by well-meaning islanders, wishing to meet her and to ask her questions (she did not mind this at all and was actually rather enjoying the warmth and joy of the people), when her eyes fell upon a woman wrapped in a dark Kierelian cloak.

The woman stood in the shadows, watching Iviana from afar, her striking face hooded beneath the cloak. Iviana thought she might have missed her entirely had it not been for that cloak.

The mysterious woman nodded to Iviana and gracefully retreated the area.

"Wait," Iviana whispered under her breath. She began pushing her way out of the crowd so that she could follow after her. It was no easy task, but eventually Iviana was able to sneak away. She hoped she was not too late.

Making her way around the quiet corner of the

tent that the lady had formerly stood beside, Iviana found the stranger was waiting for her there.

"Ah, you came. I hoped you would," the lady said in a bold, beautiful voice, "as I had no intention of wading through that rather over-zealous crowd. And... I suppose I hoped for a private meeting with you."

Iviana shifted her weight from one leg to the other, then asked, "I'm sorry. Who are you?"

The woman blinked. "Pardon me. I am called Chamaeleo most often, these days," she replied easily, then pulled back her hood to reveal long, flowing chocolate-brown hair. "I had heard that you would be here and I really only wished to catch a glimpse of you, but, when I saw you, I thought it would not hurt to speak with you." She studied Iviana. "My, you are small... and young, but you do not look helpless. No, those crystal-blue eyes are valiant. I think," she said thoughtfully, "you must be much more than you appear. You are quite capable, aren't you?"

"Capable of what?" Iviana asked, at a complete loss for understanding this strange woman.

"Oh, anything, I suppose."

Iviana shifted her weight again. "How do you know who I am?"

"The Great One told me about you... some time ago."

"He spoke to you?" Iviana asked in wonderment. "About me?"

Chamaeleo laughed. "Yes. He speaks to me often and He certainly speaks about you. How do you suppose I knew you would be here?"

"I don't know," Iviana answered. "What do you want with me?"

"Oh, heavens, nothing, my dear girl, I assure you. I just... couldn't wait to lay eyes on you. I suppose I wished for hope."

"Why?" Iviana asked her. "What has the Great One said?"

The handsome lady smiled. "I don't think it would be wise to tell you... I'm sure that's frustrating. I hope you'll forgive my impatience to see you."

"But-" Iviana tried to speak.

"I'm afraid I must go,"—she frowned—,"or I'm certain I will say something foolish and I would prefer not to spoil anything. However, I will see you again, Iviana. It has been promised."

"No, wait. I-" was all Iviana was able to mutter before the strange woman disappeared entirely from her sight; the only person left upon the little path was a tiny girl carrying a basket over her head, making her way away from Iviana. She found it odd she had not noticed the girl pass them.

&

The days that followed were fairly mundane after that occurrence. She thought often about the kindly, cloaked woman and looked for her face wherever she went, but the Isle of Knowledge offered much distraction. Most of her days were spent exploring the new island and being taught whatever each islander wished to share. These people talked a great deal, but Iviana couldn't help being grateful for the answers they provided as it was something the Isle of Dragons was not often willing to do.

Often, she found herself looking about, hoping to spot the kindly woman in the cloak, but to no avail and the island offered much to distract her.

She learned that the Greater Archipelagos stretched further than she could dream—that they were endless, or so the islanders put it. At any rate, she gathered that the land was rather vast and made up entirely of islands, small and large, and that they were not split into different kingdoms, as her world

225

was. They were entirely united, though each island was unique in itself.

As she had already learned, each island had one main leader just as the entire realm was privy one leader, the Realm Leader: Rhimesh. Iviana couldn't imagine responsibility such as that, though she was told that Rhimesh generally worked through the Island Leaders and council members. And, though she spent a portion of each year traveling to various islands, most of her work was done from the capital island: the Isle of Dragons, through correspondence. Thanks to the dragons, this was a fairly speedy process, though the further-most regions were generally a little behind on news.

Iviana also learned simpler things, such as the art of weaving. On one of the last days of her trip, a wrinkled, tan lady with gray hair and colorful clothes had taken her by the arm and pulled Iviana along while mumbling something about the most important skill every islander should be proficient at. This was the one thing Iviana truly did not care for at first. She found her sword-wielding hands were very clumsy with this sort of thing and the straw she was supposed to use was slippery and stubborn. However, Iviana decided that if she were to keep up the practice, she could be a skillful weaver and, if not, it did provide plenty of time for thought.

When Iviana was finally forced to say her goodbyes to the affectionate people, she nearly cried. She could only hope that, someday, the Isle of Dragons would treat her as this people did. Every person on the Isle of Knowledge came to send her off with a big farewell, covering her with garlands of flowers and placing blossoms and good-luck herbs in her hair. Iviana felt it was a shame that most of these would be lost in the water on her way back, but Naii pointed to the sky behind them, revealing the Great Tragor flying toward them. The sight of her dragon eased Iviana's heart and helped her to find the courage to leave these dear people and return to the Isle of Dragons.

⌘17⌘

"DO YOU REALLY miss it so terribly, Ivi? Did you even miss your friends here at all while you were away?" Nimua asked while she sat in Iviana's bedroom a few mornings later on a rare rainy day. She was absently reading a book while Iviana and Naii worked on their weaving.

"Of course I did," Iviana answered, "but for different reasons."

"That's fine—as long as you missed *me*," Nimua said in jest, winking at Iviana.

Naii chuckled at her daughter.

"Naii," Iviana started thoughtfully.

"Yes," she replied over her weaving.

"What was my mother like?" Iviana asked.

Naii concentrated on what her hands were doing for a time, making Iviana wonder if she would receive an answer. At last, Naii remarked, "Tasia wasn't much like you."

Iviana stopped her weaving and looked at the woman. That wasn't what she had expected.

Naii looked up, saw her expression and smiled a little. "That's not altogether a bad thing. She was very internal... and shy. She never would have thought about touching a sword, let alone using it... but I know she was looking forward to you, very much."

"So she was pregnant with me when she left?"

"Not that I know of, but she dreamed of having a daughter. In fact, she had already chosen quite another name for you all those years ago..." The woman smiled warmly. "I like Iviana better."

"Really? What was it?" Iviana asked in earnest.

Naii pursed her lips together, then answered, "Barkyn."

Iviana grimaced. "That's awful."

Naii and Nimua giggled, making Iviana chuckle as well.

When they settled, Iviana asked, "What do you think happened? Why did I end up with Naphtali?" Iviana wanted to know so badly and she figured Naii was her only hope at even the slightest clue.

Naii sighed. "To tell you the truth, I don't know. Before you came, I always hoped they had found a happy place to live in your realm." She paused and seemed to have some thought in her mind. She said aloud, "You were very lucky to have been raised by my mother."

The shadow that had been cast across Iviana's face vanished. "I know," she said. "Naphtali was wonderful."

"Sappy..." Nimua said under her breath and sighed.

"Ah!" Iviana exclaimed and laughed despite her shock.

"Really, Nimua, who raised you?" Naii declared, half laughing and trying to beat Nimua with the basket she was weaving. Nimua defended herself with her book, making Iviana laugh all the more.

The three refocused on what they'd been doing until Iviana sighed and looked about the white, white room.

"I don't suppose we could change any of this?" she asked, gesturing about the room. "Add some color? Some life?"

"You don't like it?" Naii asked.

"It's not bad... there's just so much... white."

"Oh, Mother...," Nimua spoke with pleading

eyes, "can we?"

"It is supposed to be a guest house," Naii said. "And it's expected to house other guests from time to time." After a moment she continued, "I think I could pull a few strings."

The next few days entailed the three women furnishing the room with ferns, small potted trees and sunflowers. They covered the walls and ceiling with earthy colored drapes of greens and browns. Nimua and Iviana set up a little still fountain in a corner of the room that held blossomed lily pads. There was moss over planks of wood on the window sills with troughs of flowers on the ground beneath them; there were even flowers and vines dripping out of the golden, spiraling, iron-barred bird cage enclosing the colorful, tody bird Naii bestowed upon Iviana as a pet.

When they were finished, Brenna stopped in to see the finished product. She decided the room should have a swing made with vines so she built one with a wooden seat and hung it in a corner of the room.

"There," she said, "now, it looks just like the forest."

Iviana offered a satisfied smile and plopped herself on the bed. "I never could have done this on my own, that's certain."

Soon after, Nimua and Brenna offered to teach Iviana how to prepare time-honored island foods using her wood-fired brick oven; Iviana had never cooked over anything but an open fire or fireplace and she heartily agreed. Though she learned to bake breads, make soups and warm seasoned fruits and vegetables with it, Iviana eventually found that the islanders rarely used the oven for much outside of that. Though they enjoyed cheeses and gooey, buttery cakes from time to time, their diet consisted of mostly raw fruits and vegetables.

When Nimua and Brenna felt Iviana had ascertained nearly all there was to know about what one provided in a meal in the Greater Archipelagos, Iviana invited Darist, Nico, Leilyn, and her two cooking tutors into her little house for a traditional island lunch.

Iviana heaved the kitchen table out onto her back patio for the occasion—she had learned that, though the islanders lounged on pillows and took food from trays during the nightly banquets, other meals were treated differently and included a table and chairs—where everyone gathered, while she laid out the large array of food she had prepared. When she and helpful Darist were finished setting up the table, gleeful cries went up all around for her tasty looking meal and nearly all complimented her on her efforts.

Iviana stepped into the house for a moment and Leilyn—who had been invited only because Iviana hoped to win a better opinion from her—stole the moment to say, "These rolls could use a little help, don't you think?" She batted her eyes at Darist, waiting for an answer.

He took a bite of Iviana's roll. "Mmm... no, I can't agree with you there. These are pretty incredible. Who knew a girl with a sword could learn to bake as well as I do." He smirked at those at the table.

Leilyn was put out by his statement, but had to object. "Oh, no, Darist. No one is a match for your baking."

"Maybe you're right," he said, but took another bite. "Naw, these are delicious."

Leilyn sat back in her seat, arms folded and a frown set on her face.

Suddenly Iviana screamed from inside the house and all but Leilyn rushed to where she was in the kitchen.

"What's the matter?" Nico, the first one at her side, exclaimed.

"What is *that?*" Iviana asked and pointed to a creepy looking creature with several long legs on the floor next to her.

Nico had been very near it and squealed as he hopped away. A moment passed before he added, "That was embarrassing."

Darist patted him on the back.

"That's a sporrick spider," Brenna replied easily," and the largest one I've ever seen." She involuntarily took a step back.

"That thing's awful looking," Nimua added.

"We should kill it," Leilyn said after coming in to see what the commotion was about.

"Agreed. Darist, you do it!" Nimua said, pushing him toward it.

He laughed, saying, "I'm not touching it."

"No!" Brenna cried. "It's harmless and you all know it."

"Does it bite... or anything?" Iviana asked.

"It can," Brenna replied, "but only if sincerely harassed. They usually just run. It's odd this one hasn't taken off yet—must be too stunned. In fact, it's odd that it's here at all. I thought the things had been made extinct on our island."

"What do you mean?" Iviana asked her.

"Well, they were all over the place years ago.

Sometimes they would creep into our homes, but not too often. Still, nobody liked them and you really can't blame them. They're not the most... comfortable looking things. Anyway, Kurnin *really* didn't care for them and thought they should be made extinct in all the Greater Archipelagos. Many agreed with him, as the bites can make you ill and many children were having nightmares about them. So, Kurnin rounded up those who agreed with him and they teamed up on ridding the whole island of them." She laughed. "Obviously, we have plenty of time on our hands. Anyway, now our island is supposed to be 'sporrick free,' but it didn't catch on with the rest of the realm, so I suppose it was only a matter of time before they made their way back on the Isle of Dragons."

Iviana supposed they couldn't survive a trip through the ocean. Then she remembered that she had flown with Tragor on the way back from the Isle of Knowledge. She did not comment on this, however. She preferred to not have Kurnin find that she may be responsible for bringing back the thing that he had worked so hard to be rid of. She knelt down on the floor to study the creature. It had a large, chubby body covered in deep purple fur and it truly was one of the most alarming little creatures she had ever seen. She stood quickly.

"Brenna? Do you mind... uh, getting it out of here?"

"What? The girl who fights off strange men with a sword can't handle a little spider?" Darist teased.

"Little?" Nico reminded.

Brenna sighed. "Get me a cup."

Iviana followed orders and watched as Brenna scooped the spider into the cup.

"Take it far away, Brenna!" Nimua yelled.

Everyone laughed as Brenna escorted the huntsman outside.

After that, they all went back to finish the meal they had started and, after having been loosened up by the spider incident, they all began to enjoy themselves. Even Leilyn, who had continued casting glares at Iviana since the day they journeyed to the waterfall, seemed to become more amicable. Truth be told, things had been awkward between Nico, Leilyn and Iviana. Iviana assumed Nico never really understood what happened that day or where he stood with her, so he only cast curious eyes on her from time to time, as if trying to read her. Leilyn looked at Iviana as if she knew what was in her mind and it offended her. Sometimes the looks made Iviana feel as though she was really the type of person

Leilyn thought she was. Even so, Leilyn seemed to have become comfortable in Iviana's little home this day and Iviana hoped that would help their relationship.

At one point, Nimua began gathering the empty plates, refusing to let Iviana help her. She did, however, allow Darist to help, as it was clear he would not be swayed.

It was some time before Iviana realized the two had not returned. Nico was telling the young women that remained on the patio yet another tale of his underwater heroics and Iviana thought he would not notice if she went inside to see what was keeping Nimua and Darist.

When she entered the kitchen, the dishes sat clean on her counter, but the two were nowhere to be seen. Iviana thought it was odd that they should leave without saying goodbye. She went to the door to go out and see if there was any sign of them, but before she could open it, she heard the voices of the two on the other side.

"I remember thinking how beautiful you looked that day," Iviana heard Darist say quietly.

Nimua laughed. "We were five!" she said.

"Still, it's what I was thinking," Darist said.

There was a small silence before Darist began, "Do you ever think that we-"

"Don't, Darist," Nimua interrupted him.

It was quiet.

Darist tried again. "I don't understand-"

"Darist, I said don't—just *don't*."

"Nimua, I've cared for you for such a long time. I always thought you felt the same way."

Iviana pulled away from the door then. Hearing the gloominess in Darist's voice, she didn't want to hear Nimua's reply. She also realized she was eavesdropping, again, though she hadn't meant to.

She began to walk back through her bedroom and out onto the patio, when she heard a scream from where she had just been. Quickly, she ran back through the house and threw open the door to find Darist sitting on the ground looking at his leg.

"Oh, Ivi, that nasty sporrick bit Darist!" Nimua shrieked. "Is he going to die?!"

Iviana grabbed her friend by the shoulder. "If he is, do you want him to hear you like this?"

Nimua shook her head and settled herself. Not sure about this, Iviana knelt down to look at the bite. "How you feeling?" Iviana asked Darist when she noticed his face looked funny.

"Oh, I'm fine," he said cloudily. "Only a spider

bite."

Iviana raised an eyebrow. He looked like he was sweating. "Are you sure-"

Darist fell to the ground.

"Nooo!" Nimua screamed.

Brenna, Nico and Leilyn finally came through the door from the back patio. They all looked surprised to find Darist on the ground with Nimua bawling on the front steps.

Leilyn fell upon Darist and cried, "Iviana, what have you done?"

Brenna knelt, seeing the bite on Darist's leg. "It was the huntsman," she said calmly.

Iviana pulled Leilyn off Darist's form and looked at his chest. "He's breathing." She leaned down to listen to his heartbeat. It was racing a little, but that meant—"He's fine. He's alive, Nimua," she informed her friend.

"Of course he's alive," Brenna said with a little humor in her voice. "It was just a sporrick spider. Their bites aren't deadly. I'm guessing he fainted. That's one of the side effects of the sporrick's bite sometimes."

Iviana smiled and felt his forehead. "Ooh, he's burning up. Lets get him inside."

&

"Am I dead?" Darist asked a while later.

Iviana chuckled. "Yes."

Darist offered a dimpled grin. "Oh, Ivi, I thought you were an angel."

Iviana grinned and gave him the little punch that Nimua would have given him if she were there. As it was, everyone else had gone to the evening banquet, upon Iviana's orders. She'd wanted him to be able to sleep off the fever.

"Hey, I think Nim's rubbing off on you," Darist said and rubbed his arm. Suddenly he gave a little "arg" and held his hands to his head. "That hurts."

"What does? Your head?"

He nodded. "Feels like someone hit it with a shovel."

Iviana placed her hand to his head. Using her gift, she looked into his body. Other than a slight fever, a racing heart and a bad headache, everything was fine. She removed her hand. "I think I can come up with something for that."

She went out the patio door and returned with a leafy plant a few minutes later. Holding it out to him she said, "Get that down, if you can."

Darist took the plant and sniffed it doubtfully. "Heffesplis?" he asked.

"Is that what it's called?" Iviana asked innocently.

"Yes," Darist said unhappily. "It's not going to taste good. How do you know it'll help if you don't even know what it's called?"

"My gift." She smiled and patted his head. "Get it down," she said, leaving the room to fetch him a glass of water. Upon her return, Darist was gagging on what he'd just swallowed. "Here." She handed him the glass. He accepted and quickly emptied it.

"I don't feel any better," he managed to choke out.

"You will. Just wait." She held her hand to his head and willed the herb to do its work. Just as she opened her eyes, she saw a purple glow under her touch.

"What was that?" Darist asked, looking into her face with surprise.

"Nothing."

He eyed her, but said nothing. Then he pulled his leg out from under the blankets on Iviana's bed and observed the wound. "Doesn't look all that bad. I think it was just a surprise and uh..." he coughed, "that's why I passed out."

Iviana's eyes gleamed with the giggle she was

holding back. "I think it was more the effects of the bite that knocked you out, rather than any reaction of yours," she reassured him.

He grinned. "Of course it was."

They were quiet a moment and Darist spoke unhappily, "I guess she disliked the conversation we were having as much as I did."

"Who?"

"The spider."

"Oh."

Darist looked at her. "I really do care about her."

"I suppose you're referring to Nimua this time," Iviana commented.

Darist looked confused a moment. "Oh!" He cast her another dimpled grin. "Yes. Nimua."

Iviana laughed and nodded. Then her face expressed her guilt.

"What's the matter?" Darist asked her, looking worried.

"I'm sorry, Darist. I sort of accidentally overheard a part of your conversation."

He relaxed. "That's alright, Ivi. Better you than anyone else, I suppose."

"Why?"

He gave her a long look as if he was trying to locate the answer himself. "I don't know. Because you're Ivi, I suppose."

Iviana laughed. "Alright. I'll accept that."

Suddenly, Darist's eyes brightened. "I just realized the ache in my head is gone."

Iviana placed her hand on his head once again. "Your fever's gone too."

"That was fast," Darist said. He looked at her, fascinated.

"There are lots of Healers here. Surely you're not impressed with what a little herb can do."

Darist looked at her. "I know it wasn't just the herb."

She turned red.

"I've never been tended by a Healer, nor have I seen it done before. The Healers like people to stay out of their business. At least the one here does."

"I don't know if–"

"We should tell anyone you used your healing? No, I don't think we should, either."

Iviana nodded. "Thanks, Darist."

Darist grabbed her hand. "Thank you, Ivi."

Iviana removed her hand from his and looked guilty again.

"What is it this time?" Darist asked.

"I think it may have been my fault you received the bite in the first place," she said.

"Sheesh, Ivi. I know you're a sweet girl and all, but I don't think you need to start accepting blame for a spider's actions. Unless, of course, you have some gift with animals you haven't told us about."

"I know, but I think I might be the one who brought it back to the island when Tragor flew me home from the Isle of Knowledge."

Darist chuckled. "Good. Then you undid the silly thing Kurnin tried to do."

"It's not funny, Darist! Last I heard, the man dislikes me enough. Besides, what if the spider bite had been really harmful and you *died?* I would be responsible for that."

"Ivi, I'm not dead," Darist said plainly. "I'm *fine* thanks to you. My head doesn't even hurt anymore." He put his hand under her chin and made her raise her head. "And who *cares* what Kurnin thinks?"

She batted his hand away and let a smile creep onto her face, deciding he was right.

Just then, they heard someone outside on the patio and peered up. It was Leilyn and she looked pale.

"You're alright?" Leilyn asked Darist sweetly.

"Yes, Leilyn, I'm just fine," he answered with his normal grin, as if no one should have been worrying about him in the first place.

"I'm glad," she said with a smile. "Goodnight, Darist."

Before turning to go, she cast Iviana a more solid glare than she ever had before and walked into the night.

Iviana sighed, but smiled to herself. *And who cares what Leilyn thinks?*

ɮ18 beta

IVIANA WAS TRULY enjoying time with her new friends. She was beginning to feel as though she could make a home in the Greater Archipelagos and it felt good to know there wasn't a threat of being sent back to Kaern anymore.

"If they were going to do it, they would have done it already," Nimua told her when she'd asked.

There was always the illusive "they." She never really understood what that meant. The council? The island? The entirety of the Greater Archipelagos? She had given up long ago.

There was one thing tugging at her subconscious, however. No one had ever asked her to use her healing. Some time ago, Naii had claimed her gift was needed, but if that was true, was it that they still didn't trust her? She willed herself not to think that way... She couldn't if she was going to make her home here. Perhaps they had merely forgotten about her healing entirely. *Oh well,* she said to herself, deciding that if she was ever to hear of a need, she would offer her service.

But when occasions arose, she did not. Something held her back, and, though she was fairly certain it was fear, she did not want to face it.

There were many things to distract her. One such preoccupation was watching Darist fall harder for Nimua while Leilyn glared at Iviana every time Darist paid Iviana any attention. Iviana wondered how Leilyn could keep this up and somehow never realize where his true feelings lay. Nimua appeared not to notice any of this, though Iviana felt it must be impossible she truly did not. Even so, she chose not to pry. Romance did not interest her much; it only bothered her when it caused someone to dislike her.

Nico's affection for Iviana made up for Leilyn's dislike. Luckily, he had not been too forward, but always there were small things that reminded Iviana she couldn't be too friendly with him. Nimua had continued to encourage him to do little things here and there until Iviana assured her she would never care for Nico that way. Nimua told her she was foolish to not at least enjoy the situation, but said she understood.

When Nico finally pulled her aside just as the banquet was beginning one night, Iviana discovered how seriously he was thinking without Nimua's help. He guided her away from the Grand Pavilion where they were not so easily heard.

"What's going on, Nico?" Iviana asked, naive to his intent.

"Ivi, I... was hoping you could guess," he muttered, scratching his ash-blonde head nervously.

"Guess what?" she asked, bewildered.

He shook his head. "Never mind." His blue eyes looked like they might pop out of his head, he was so intense. "I just, well—ever since I met you that day on the beach—I think you're really... special." He rubbed his hand through his hair as if he had to keep his hands busy.

"Oh..." Iviana replied. "Um, thank you..." She had never been in this situation and wasn't positive she knew what he was getting at.

"Well..." he started and drew closer to her. "I'd like to know whether or not you feel the same about me." He was looking deeply into her eyes.

Iviana gulped. "Huh?" She didn't like where this was going and she could sense something going on in the Grand Pavilion now that the banquet had begun, but she couldn't hear anything from this distance.

Nico took yet another step closer, his tall frame towering over her. "I would really like to get to know you better," he said. "And to one day marry you," he added softly.

But Iviana was struggling to hear what was going on in the Grand Pavilion. It had something to do with Healers. "Wait, I'm sorry. Did you hear that?" she asked him and took a few steps closer to the hall, straining to hear.

He wrapped a hand a little too tightly around her wrist, forcing her back and said in a deep voice, "Please don't walk away while we're talking about this."

His grip on her wrist and dominating voice were irritating and she needed to hear what was going on. It was completely silent except for one voice and it was not Rhimesh's, as she would have expected.

He turned her around and took her by the hands. She looked up and finally saw how intense his eyes were, and the emotion they held. She understood what this was about, though she hadn't heard his earlier declaration.

She took off running.

"I'm sorry, Nico!" she yelled back at him as she ran up to one of the white columns of the hall and listened for the lone voice.

Nico did not follow.

"We have invited the most gifted and experienced Healers of the Greater Archipelagos to look into the matter," Iviana heard an unfamiliar male voice say, "but we ask that you keep her in your thoughts and prayers and that you do not disturb her home for any reason. Our leader must gain whatever rest she can. Our Island Leader, Kurnin, will be available to answer any of your questions. Thank you all for your concern."

With that, the voice ceased, but the hush did not. Iviana wasn't certain who or what the speaker had been referring to, but she had a sick feeling in the pit of her stomach when murmurs quietly began to form and their volume rose. Iviana waited until the islanders began to stir again to run to where her friends were.

"Where were you?" Nimua asked, concerned.

"She ran off with Nico," Leilyn put in, watching Darist's face.

"What?!" Nimua squealed. "I thought you told me you weren't interested?"

"I'm not!" Iviana defended. "He just wanted to... talk to me about something. But wait, I didn't hear what that man was talking about. What's going on?"

"Poor Rhimesh," Nimua answered, her brows furrowed. "She is ill and our Healer hasn't been able to help her.

"If they're announcing it at banquet, it's very serious," Darist explained gently.

"They've just called in the best Healers, though," Brenna added positively. "Surely, she'll be better soon."

ॐ

Days passed and the islands of the Greater Archipelagos waited, but the Healers refused to convey any information. This only caused more tension in the day-to-day life of the realm. All were quiet, trying to pay respect to their Realm Leader in uttered prayers to the Great One. Iviana rarely saw anyone but Naii and Nimua—though she did make regular visits to see Tragor, who was always eager to see her—as no one was in the state of mind to busy themselves with delights while the well-honored woman was ill. Even the nightly banquets were canceled until further notice. This, at least, made it so Iviana did not have to face Nico, though Iviana was informed by Nimua, who heard from Darist, who heard from Leilyn, who heard from Brenna, who heard from Nico, that he was miserable and would never find room in his heart to love again. Naii rolled her eyes at that.

Just as the people were beginning to come out of their homes, the Healers released news that the beloved Realm Leader was not recovering and over the weeks that followed, she grew worse. One night after the island had been summoned for a meeting, another announcement was made. Iviana and her friends were huddled around Naii as if gleaning courage from the older woman. No one could be certain what the announcement would entail, but stomachs were in knots as they waited.

It was clear that when someone had been Realm Leader for almost a hundred years, it was generally hoped that, that person would remain so for some time longer. They are the one on whom the entire realm comes to rely, lean on and trust and it is no great affair to accept a new Realm Leader. Every island in the Greater Archipelagos waited that night, for whatever news was to be relayed by their Island Leader, hoping that it may contain that which they prayed to hear.

At last, Kurnin, entered the banquet hall of the Isle of Dragons and stood upon the platform. During the short time Iviana had been in the realm, she had learned that this was a rarity: the man did not publicly speak often. His face was unreadable and he stood with hands laid perfectly at his sides, facing the islanders before him head on.

"I thank you for attending this meeting tonight. It will not be long." He paused. "You have been made aware for some time now that the esteemed leader of our realm, Rhimesh, has fallen ill. I thank you also for your prayers and thoughts of well-being for her. Our own Healer, along with the most talented Healers in all the archipelagos, have been working together to relieve her from this malady.

"Last night, Rhimesh requested that we arrange a Time of Waiting... that we may find and recognize the next Realm Leader of the Greater Archipelagos."

He was interrupted by gasps, moans and thunderous murmurs. He waited patiently until granted the opportunity to continue.

"As you know, it is customary to send Seekers to find the next Realm Leader, but as this gift has not occurred in any of our people since the days of Latos, it is the Time of Waiting that we will utilize in hope that our Seers will be shown who is to replace Rhimesh when she passes."

There were more outbursts, but the man was

eventually able to finish with, "Tomorrow evening, when the sun has set, we will gather around the Great Fire, as will our sister islands, and we will wait upon the Great Being to show us the way. Please see me or any member of my council for whatever questions and concerns you may have."

After the Island Leader stepped down from the podium and out of the hall, the people openly conversed and bickered among themselves. It was a deep chorus of mild chaos as everyone squabbled over whether or not this was really happening. Naii explained to Iviana that people so rarely ever died from illness in the Greater Archipelagos, that it was a great blow when it did occur. The Healers were usually able to take care of whatever ailed the islanders and this was a strange case. For it to have struck the Realm Leader was a sad blow.

"So there have been no Seekers after my grandfather?" Iviana asked her, bewildered.

"No, there have not. Some wonder if it is because of him that the gift has not been bestowed again, but I believe the Great One is merciful. It seems unlike Him to me. I cannot say why the gift has become extinct."

ଞ

There was much for Iviana to think about as she lay in bed that night. The fresh, night air lightly blew through her open windows as she gazed at the brilliant night sky. It shown just as brightly as any other night, but her heart was so heavy, it appeared darker somehow. Rhimesh had shown her kindness and had been one of the first that seemed to offer her trust. What could be ailing her that was *incurable?* She had never come across anything like that... except in Naphtali. It had been too late for her to fully understand what had stolen her mentor's life.

If ever there was a time she wished to offer her services as a Healer, it was now. It seemed they believed Rhimesh's cause was hopeless so there would be nothing to lose in allowing her to at least take a look and see if she could come up with something they may have missed. Even so, she was afraid of appearing arrogant or impertinent in wishing to try to do what even the best Healers could not achieve. Perhaps she *was* arrogant... but no. There was something inside of her... mere faith? A glimmer? A quiet voice? She couldn't put her finger on it, but she wanted to have a look at

Rhimesh, at least. She had learned so much about the herbs and plants on the island. Surely there would be one that could do something for her. She huffed and turned over on her bed. Tomorrow she would speak to Kurnin.

♋19♋

IVIANA SPOTTED KURNIN along the island's main path. Where he was going she had no idea, but if she could just catch him now, before he became engaged with something else, it would make this much easier. It was rare that one received the luxury of catching him alone.

Making her way toward him, her mind was fighting her. It was very, *very* hard to forget what Kurnin had said that day at Rhimesh's home as she had never received an apology or even an explanation. She comforted herself in the memory of what had happened only the other day.

She and Nimua had been traveling along this path when they came upon Kurnin. When he passed them, he offered a curt nod—something he had not formerly done before. Iviana knew it was a long shot,

257

but she hoped it meant he was warming to her. It had to.

Besides, surely he would be willing to try anything to make the beloved Realm Leader well.

She drew beside him, but was short of breath after jogging to meet him.

"Iviana, can I help you with something?" the Island Leader asked her. "Are you quite alright?" He displayed some concern, but she wasn't certain it was for her.

"I," she struggled to speak past her breathing. "I was hoping to see Rhimesh."

"Ah, that is out of the question. She is resting." He continued hurrying down the path.

Iviana ran after him. "But I was hoping... perhaps I could... take a look at her, as a Healer, and see if there is anything I can do."

He shook his head and answered politely. "I understand you want to help, but our greatest Healers have an eye on her. I don't think you'll be needed." He spoke to her as if she was a small child.

"Please," she begged, "might I at least try? If she is lost then I could not do anymore harm and–"

"I have given you my answer," he said sternly. "Besides, I would have to speak with the council before I allow you to use your gift."

Iviana felt as though she'd been punched in the stomach. She could not believe that they had not spoken of the matter already. Her healing was important to her and it shocked her that they had not even given it a thought.

She knew very well that she should let it go, but she had to try once more. "Could you?" she asked meekly.

Kurnin haulted, faced her and took a chilly tone. "There is reason you have not been granted permission. You may as well know that you are not a trusted member of this community at this time—I doubt if you ever will be—and Rhimesh is the last person I would allow you to come in contact with right now. For all we know, you're the one who cursed her with this wretched illness. I will ask you once to return to your hut and to remain there until the Time of Waiting. You may choose to do so, or I will be forced to command it of you. It is up to you."

Iviana was speechless. Tears were stinging the edges of her eyes, threatening to overflow. The man waited for her to make a move toward her home. She knew she had no choice but to go. Slowly, she started and immediately the man turned his back on her and went on his way.

Iviana's eyes threatened to overflow with the

tears that had been brimming a moment before but she refused to give the man the satisfaction of shed tears. She ran toward her hut. All she wanted to do was to run inside and hide herself away. She was humiliated.

Just as she reached the little walk up to her hut, she noticed Nimua and Darist turn toward her from the hut's doorstep.

"Oh, there you are. We were just coming to— Ivi, what's the matter?" Nimua asked. She rushed up to Iviana and took hold of her hands.

Iviana struggled to speak without crying, but she managed, "I just—I just wanted to help. I felt something... urging me to."

"Help with what, dear?" Nimua asked her sympathetically.

Iviana waited a moment before answering. Pulling herself together, she explained, "I asked Kurnin if I could try my healing on Rhimesh," she explained.

Darist stepped forward, an angry expression setting on his face. "And?"

Iviana continued, "He said that I am not trustworthy and he as good as commanded that I return to my home for the day. He practically accused me of making her sick."

"That's what I was afraid of," Darist muttered grimly, hands clenched into fists.

"Oh, Ivi, that is so wrong. It's so unjust," Nimua said. She embraced Iviana and drew her inside. They sat down on the chairs in the kitchen and Nimua continued, "I could tell, when I asked my mother, that she was upset by whatever they had discussed in the council meetings about you, but I hoped by *now* they would have *changed.* Rhimesh even allowed you to visit the Isle of Knowledge. *She* obviously trusts you. It's almost like what happened to-" She stopped short.

"My parents," Iviana finished for her. "...and Naphtali. I don't think they ever intend to let me live outside my father's shadow. At least they haven't forced me to leave, I suppose..."

"Not yet anyway," Darist added bitterly. He seemed as though he could barely keep his anger in check.

"Yes..." Iviana answered. She knew then that she might never be able to let her guard down in this land. They were never going to lower theirs.

"We trust you, Ivi: your friends. I more than trust you; I adore you and hope to be more like you," Nimua spoke with feeling.

"Thank you." Iviana forced a smile.

She felt so out of place and alone.

∞

Iviana, Nimua and Darist made their way to where the waiting ritual was to take place—where it always had taken place. Nimua explained that the Time of Waiting consisted of all the islanders gathered together to wait upon the Great One to show a Seer whatever knowledge was needed. These meetings were used for many situations, but had only been used for finding the Realm Leader since the Seekers had become extinct. Nimua and Darist had attended the meetings rarely, but each had been a unique situation and was something not easily forgotten.

"What do those who aren't Seers do?" Iviana had asked Nimua.

"We pray to the Great One and we wait."

"How long does it take?"

"It has never gone past the rising of the sun."

"So, yes," Darist cut in, "we could be there for a while."

They approached a large bonfire on the beach, meant for giving light and warmth through the night. Over half the island was already there, gathered in a circle around it. Seers and those of higher rank were seated in the center ring surrounding the fire and everyone else fanned out from there. Iviana and Darist were a few heads behind where Nimua was with Naii in the center. Whispers sounded all over, as no one wanted to be disrespectful by speaking too loudly on this occasion, but the collaboration of whisperers ended up sounding like a rushing river and Kurnin was forced to shout over the crowd.

"You all know what this night entails," Kurnin began.

Not really, Iviana thought.

"Our goal is to provide time for our Seers to be shown who the next Realm Leader of the Greater Archipelagos is to be and we will remain patient until we have been granted an answer. Without further ado, let us call upon the Great One."

Iviana was ready for the noise level to rise tremendously after that, but it seemed Kurnin had meant that they should call upon the Great One in their minds. The wind blowing through the crowd and the crackling fire was all that could be heard.

Alright, she could do this...

Iviana found it difficult however. She didn't

know this Great One very well and it was hard to know what should be said to Him.

Uh, Great One... she began, *would You please show us who will replace Rhimesh as Realm Leader?* Her eyes had been closed, but they opened now. That was all she had. If this was supposed to go on for a while, well, she really didn't relish the idea of standing all night with nothing to say but "please." She tried again.

You see all these people here, all these people all over the realm of the Greater Archipelagos? They're all waiting on You. They actually trust You. I can only dream that they will ever trust me even a little. You're lucky... but I guess You've earned it. Anyway, Rhimesh is ill and dying and I wish I could help her... I wish I could use the Great Gift you gave me, but–I'm sorry–they won't let me try.

Have I ever thanked you for the gift? I suppose not. I'm not even certain You gave it to me, but when I touch the greenery that has healing in it, I think I can feel You. So, thank you. I suppose this isn't the point of all this, though.

Oh, please, show us.

Some time later, Iviana looked up at Darist who looked back at her and gave a little shrug, then went back to his prayers. *How can these people do this for so long?* she wondered.

Great One, where are you??

She opened her eyes again and was underwater. She was breathing underwater and she was in the place Nico had taken her some time ago. It was no longer dark; sunlight shown through the water, warming her where she was.

A melodious, booming voice seemed to emanate from the glittering light. "Sweet Ivi, you are never alone. I am waiting for you. Seek. *Seek Me.*"

The voice's presence was so intense that Iviana became heavy with the weight of the words spoken to her. She would have sunk to the bottom of the ocean, but the next thing she knew, the Time of Waiting surrounded her again. Iviana glanced about, wondering if anyone had noticed anything, but they were all standing still, waiting on the Great One.

What was that? Iviana asked herself or the Great One; she wasn't sure which. She was sure, however, that the voice that had spoken to her was the voice of the Great One Himself and He was powerful. No, He was power itself and so much more. One thing she knew now, He wanted her to seek Him. She had felt the intensity of His desire and she promised she would, even though she was uncertain as to what that meant.

It was nearly dawn when a messenger came saying that not one island had reported a Seer receiving an answer. Darist whispered to her that it had never been this close to sunrise before they gained what knowledge was needed.

Kurnin spoke, looking tired and haggard. "I will encourage all of you to speak aloud to the Great One with whatever strength you have left."

It still was not the rocketing volume Iviana originally expected, for the crowd was very tired, but it was louder than Iviana had supposed a group of people who had been silent for hours could be. She did not call aloud however. After her experience, she didn't know why, but she had nothing to say. Iviana felt assured that everything would be fine—that they would acquire the answers they needed. The powerful Voice was listening and would not let them down.

Abruptly, Nimua stepped forward and turned to her mother, face shining with something Iviana couldn't identify. "Mother, He showed me."

Naii looked shocked. "What did you see, Nim?"

Nimua searched the crowd until she found Iviana's face. Her eyes were sparkling. "Ivi."

All was still and silent.

"She had the green fire of the Seeker burning

through her body. She was glorious and she will be able to use the Seeker's gift to find the next Realm Leader of the Greater Archipelagos."

"Are you certain of this?" a woman from the council asked doubtfully.

Nimua spoke with an authority Iviana had never heard from her before. It reminded her of Naii. "I haven't the slightest doubt. I feel His presence here, even now. He's been here the whole time." A small, magical laugh escaped her lips.

With rather severe expression, everyone turned to where Iviana was standing beside Darist and her face turned the scarlet it had on the first night she attended the banquet.

"Iviana," Naii called to her, "will you join us here." She motioned for Iviana to come to her. Iviana guessed it was so she could protect her from the same accusing eyes that were accusing her own daughter. Darist hooked her arm through his and escorted her to the center ring.

Kurnin, along with another man from the council, walked up to the young women beside Naii. "Is this some plot you ladies have cooked up?" Kurnin accused. "Nimua does not even have a gift, let alone the gift of the Seer. Did you really think you could pull the wool over my eyes like this?" His voice was fully embittered.

Naii stepped between him and the girls, mere inches from his face, and snapped, "Watch your tongue, Kurnin. You will save your accusations for the council meeting this afternoon. Nimua is correct. The Great One is here. This is no plot, no trick. There is no wool here."

Kurnin stepped back, eyes filled with rage. "As you say, woman. We will settle this tomorrow."

Naii turned to Darist. "Will you escort the girls to Iviana's? I know they can take care of themselves, but it doesn't hurt to have extra friends about."

In complete silence, the three walked back the way they had come. When they reached the house, Darist said he'd be sleeping on the hammock on the back patio while the young women slept in Iviana's room. They were completely exhausted and slept through the entire day, making up for the sleep they had lost during the Time of Waiting.

When Iviana finally awoke, it was nearly dark again and Nimua and Darist had already left. Sometime that day, the council had met and decided her fate. She didn't need to ask what the decision had been. She already knew. Iviana would never be allowed to use her gifts. The Healer, Seer, Seeker wanted to cry. Instead, she grabbed a hunk of bread

for her empty stomach and determined her course for
Seer's Hill.

ಶ20ೞ

IN THE DARK, it was an awkward trek up the mountain, but as always, it was never as dark here as it might have been in her home world. The sky was vibrant enough and she chose not to take a torch with her. She did not want anyone to know her whereabouts. Below, nearly all the buildings on the island were lit. This surprised her. She would have hoped they'd all be nearing sleep, but she supposed they were as restless as she was, possibly pondering the stranger who had been brought by the dragon, Tragor.

When she finally arrived at Marquen's quiet home, he was already standing in the doorway. He waved to her and welcomed her in.

"You were expecting me?" she asked.

He nodded his head to where the brilliant dove

was perched on a window sill. He motioned for her to sit as he sat and the dove perched on his shoulder.

"What troubles you, Ivi?" Marquen asked.

"You don't know?"

"I do, but I'd like to hear what you have to say."

Iviana sighed. "You know about the Time of Waiting? I didn't see you there."

He nodded. "I know about it. I was not there physically. The islanders and I prefer to keep our distance, so I remain here. But please, tell me what you will."

Iviana longed to have Marquen explain why he would not go, but felt time was of the essence. "Nimua had a vision," she explained instead. "She said I'm a Seeker—that there is some sort of green fire burning within me. Once the words left her mouth, I knew and I could feel it: the fire, I mean. I still do and I don't think I can ignore it."

Marquen was thoughtful for a time before asking, "Have you had any dreams since you've been here; dreams that might feel different from others?"

"Yes," Iviana responded immediately. "How did you know?"

"I didn't. Tell me about it. When did this dream occur?"

She thought back. "The night I had spoken with

271

the council and told them about my healing-the same day I met you." She told him the dream.

"Do you know what it means?" he asked her.

"No... but I found out that this 'Latos' the woman in the dream spoke of is actually my great-grandfather. It's true that I'm a daughter of Latos."

"You say that half of you was missing and 'she,' I think we can safely say Aradia, was pleased to find you there, lying helpless on the beach. Think about it. What half do you think you were missing?"

"Aradia?" Iviana questioned. " The witch who killed Latos?"

"Yes," he replied simply and sat forward in his chair. "Iviana, please try to answer the question."

She racked her brain for an answer, trying to think past the shock of realizing he was right about Aradia—though she wasn't sure how she knew this—when suddenly enlightenment shown on her face.

"The Seeker: that's what I was missing at the time of the dream. Without my seeking... I am helpless?"

"I think... without your Seeker's gift, she will have her way—whatever that may be."

Iviana's stomach tensed. "But isn't she dead by now?"

"Apparently not."

"What am I expected to do then? Seek her? Or seek the future Realm Leader? I may be a Seer too, Marquen. I think I had a vision of some sort. Does that mean anything?"

He nodded and said, "It's what I thought when I first met you, but it is not the gift you need right now. Or perhaps it is, I really don't know everything. I think all that is left for you now is to follow your inner leading; follow the burning gift inside of you and our Great Friend will guide you."

"But the islanders, they will be angry. They don't trust me and what if I can't do anything after all? What if I'm still helpless even with my gift? I mean, what kind of defense can seeking provide for me should I encounter a witch?"

Marquen turned his head to look out the window and spoke, "Those who trust in the One Eternal will gain strength. They will soar high on the winds of His Spirit."

The pure white dove on Marquen's shoulder looked straight into Iviana's eyes and she felt it speak into her spirit, *I will be with you, always.*

In that moment, Iviana determined she would go and obey her call. Something like a dark veil lifted off her and she could feel the gifts inside as she never had before. All three were so strong in her and she was filled with new strength. Iviana stood to her feet. The Seeker's fire burned powerfully within, coursing through every part of her.

"Farewell, Marquen," she muttered as she marched out the door.

As she made her way down the mountain path, she spotted Nimua racing toward her. When she drew nearer, Iviana could see she was crying profusely.

"What's the matter, Nim?" She reached out and held her friend.

"Were you with Marquen?" Nimua asked. "I was just going to see him. Oh, Darist and I got into a fight—a real one this time! He says he's in love with me and he'll never speak to me again if I continue to claim I don't love him back! Isn't he wretched, Ivi?? You've got to talk to him. He'll listen to you."

Iviana was torn. Nimua had been there for her since the moment she arrived. She couldn't forgo helping her friend the one time she needed her. On the other hand, she knew she must go now. This couldn't wait. There was an urging within her and it burned.

"Nim, Nimua... I'm sorry. He shouldn't have said that. He's hurt. But look... I've got to go. I can feel the Seeker inside me now, like a fire, just like you said. It's begging me to go, with an urgency... that I can't believe I never noticed before."

"Oh, you're leaving?! Now?" Nimua sniffed. "I want to come with you!"

Iviana thought a moment, half consulting the One who was compelling her, and she knew she must go alone.

"I can't take you. I don't know what's awaiting me out there... I really don't even know where I'm going yet. I've got to place all my focus on this. It's too new."

Nimua sighed. "I understand... I wish you weren't going so soon. What if—I hate to say it—but what if I don't see you again?"

Iviana consulted again, but she wasn't sure of the answer this time. "Thank you for being such a dear friend."

Nimua smiled and hugged her. "Alright, get out of here!" she scolded in jest, wiping tears from her eyes. "Stop wasting time on this sap."

Iviana smiled halfheartedly. "Yes ma'am," she answered and went to find Tragor.

❧ 21 ❧

IVIANA WAS READY to take the turn to the dragon's lair when she felt herself pulled another direction. She obeyed and followed the fire into the dense, tropical forest she had spent so much time exploring. With the treetops managing to block the moonlight, it was almost too dark to make out where she was going, but she knew what she was here for and didn't have to go far.

Eventually, a large patch of an herb she knew well was at her left. She knelt down to steal a handful and felt the healing power pulsing through the plant. Iviana had always known this could be a powerful healer, but the island Healer did not use it nor did he know what ailment it should be used for. Everything she'd used previously had been taught her by Naphtali. She had never noticed or needed the "curative identification" part of her gift until she had come to the island.

When she had what was needed, Iviana hurried to the little hut that had been her home and changed into the clothes she had worn into this realm. She proceeded to fill her pack with the herbs, food and other odds and ends that were hers to take, firmly belting her sword into place. Looking around her earthy bedroom, she sighed and pushed back tears. This may never be her home again. Indeed, as much as it looked like her and what she and her friends had made it, it was no longer. It was a guest house and it belonged to the island once again; it had been made clear that she was not a part of this world. This could no longer remain hers even if she wasn't about to lose the faith of the islanders forever.

Her insides burned again. It was not painful, but she knew she must obey. She wondered how her grandfather had ignored his own gift. She left the little building and silently crept toward Rhimesh's home. Iviana hoped the Realm Leader hadn't been moved somewhere else because of her ailment, but as the ageless woman was dying, it seemed a foolish thing to do.

As she went, Iviana was almost spotted a few times by passersby, but stayed far away from the paths and crept slowly in the shadows. She assumed that, after what Nimua had said about her at the Time of Waiting, the islanders would care even less for her. They were probably assuming she had been apart of some conspiracy. Her own assumptions about their thoughts may or may not be true, but she supposed it would be easier not to find out. Besides, it was the middle of the night and she was carrying her traveling pack. She didn't care to answer any questions.

When she finally reached Rhimesh's hut, two pairs of islanders were guarding the front and back doors. *Alright, I'm here... but what do I do now?* she wondered. She had to hurry before anyone spotted her behind the bushes in Rhimesh's garden and before she burst from the burning she was trying to ignore for the moment. She knew she was working with precious time.

Not knowing what else to do, she was tempted to try sneaking in through a window, but just as she was about to creep out of the bushes, a large shadow fell over the house, catching the attention of the guards at the back door. Iviana smiled when she saw Tragor lead the men away from the house. She couldn't even guess how he knew she would need him, but she stole the opportunity to dash into

Rhimesh's house while the guards were distracted.

The room she entered was dimly lit. There was a fireplace burning at the far wall and Rhimesh lay alone in a large bed. Iviana crept slowly toward her, hoping the woman was asleep. She was. Iviana felt the woman's forehead and sensed a nasty curse inside the woman. She traced it to the ageless lady's stomach and, after realizing what it was, thought she would throw up. Instead, she steadied herself and pressed her hand lightly against the stomach again, wanting to confirm that it was the same thing she had felt in Naphtali's blood before she had died.

"Iviana... I'm so tired, " Rhimesh suddenly whispered to her.

"I know." Iviana wanted to cry. "But I think I can help you, if you'll let me."

"Yes, I've been waiting for you to come to me, Iviana. Why didn't you?"

"It's complicated."

Iviana turned and rummaged through her pack for the herb she had just gathered, then took a bowl from the kitchen and crushed the plant until it was smooth. Iviana was thankful when she saw the cauldron of hot water boiling in the fireplace and added a ladle of it into her bowl. She stirred it into the herb. Having poured the substance into a cup,

Iviana sat on the bed and held the Realm Leader's head up. Rhimesh drank, though it burned, and laid her head back down.

"I think that will take care of it for a while," Iviana told her. She added sadly, "but not forever. It will come to battle you again and I don't know that your body will be able to withstand it. Perhaps if I had come sooner..." She was ready to cry, but Rhimesh hushed her.

"Iviana, I thank you... for your heart and for your help." Iviana squeezed the woman's hand. "You're leaving," Rhimesh said. "I know why you must go. Good luck to you, Iviana. I will keep you in my prayers."

Iviana stood and replied, "You will be in mine as well, but rest now. You will need all the strength you can get."

She had forgotten about the guards outside. Tragor must have let them lose him for they were only a few feet away from the door when she exited the hut. They shouted when they saw her, commanding she remain where she was, but Iviana was no longer in the habit of obeying these islanders. She quickly darted around the side of the house where she gratefully met Tragor and leaped onto his back, allowing him to race her into the clouds.

"Tragor, I love you!" She hugged him hard and patted him on the back. "You're wonderful. I don't know how you knew I needed you, but I thank you."

Following the Seeker's fire, Iviana was inadvertently leading them back in the same direction from where Tragor had brought her into this world. She simply followed the gift and, next thing she knew, they were flying through a whirling vortex. It was then that Iviana realized the thing had not been a dream and she was confronted with the realization that she would not be staying in the realm of the Greater Archipelagos.

I suppose I'm not seeking the future Realm Leader, after all, Iviana thought. *Perhaps this means Rhimesh will remain well for some time, but then...* The realization she was seeking Aradia after all set in. Shaking her head, Iviana didn't want to consider that and as it turned out, she didn't have to, for they were tossed out of the speeding vortex. The strength of Tragor's wings took control, however, and they floated peacefully into the night air of Kierelia: home at last.

Iviana shouted with arms raised toward the sky, "I had no idea I would be so happy to be back!"

Breathing in air devoid of sea mist and honey,

she was rewarded by the scent of rock and dust, but was no less grateful.

Very faintly, she remembered having been in this wasteland before, with Tragor, but could not tell how long they would be in it now, as the trip to this point was less than a blur.

They traveled through the night as well as the next day until the sun set. By the time the sun's light was finally hidden, a cold fear wrapped around her being. She knew she must be close and she feared what awaited her. It didn't help that a thick smoke began to drift from Tragor's nostrils and, when she afforded a glance, his eyes were ashen. His entire body was hot to the touch, slowly warming the chill in her own. She knew he could sense Aradia as well; he did not care for the witch.

The realization hit Iviana that Tragor knew this woman far better than she did. He would have been there when the witch took the life of Iviana's great-grandfather so long ago. The thought that she was still alive made the hairs on her arms stand on end. What power had given Aradia the ability to have lived this long? Was she even human within her flesh or had she been completely stolen by her demons? If this were so, how could she, Iviana, do... whatever it was that was required of her?

Those who trust in the One Eternal will gain strength.

They passed over a heavily wooded forest and into a clearing. She no longer had to urge the dragon in the direction that was needed; he knew as well as she did.

The two landed in the clearing opposite where a small, dark shanty stood. *That's not what I expected,* she thought, but the dragon's eyes gleamed black and she had never seen him look so ferocious. This had to be the right place. Iviana moved to walk toward the shack, but the dragon blocked her way, glaring, warning.

"I have to go. You know that. I'm sorry you can't go in with me, but just... wait for me here, alright?"

He didn't budge.

"I'll call if I need you," she lied.

He didn't look convinced, but allowed her to pass.

Not knowing any other way to go about it, she boldly strode to the door of the shanty and knocked, thinking all the while that this was too easy, too simple. When no one answered, she knocked again and heard a black, impish voice speak into her being, *Enter... daughter of Latos.*

Iviana stepped back. She wasn't sure she dared, but her body still burned with the fire of her gift. She was seeking and she must continue; she refused to waste it and turn her back on the Great One as her grandfather had.

Slowly, she urged the door open and was greeted with darkness. She stepped in. When her eyes adjusted, it became apparent the one-room shack was completely empty but for a thick, terrifying presence that resided in the atmosphere. Her eyes caught on something: a latch on the floor. She knelt beside it and found there was a square door in the dusty, wooden floor.

Unlatching it, Iviana found a square-shaped tunnel that plummeted further than her eyes could see, with a ladder crawling down the side of one of the walls. The burning of the Seeker was aflame inside of her and she was shaking with it and with fear. Surely, she would not have to climb down this dark tunnel. It reminded her too much of her time spent in the cave's abyss when she'd found the door to the Greater Archipelagos. She felt she had lived a lifetime since then.

Prolonging the inevitable for some time, she eventually forfeited.

"A light?" she queried doubtfully.

Suddenly, there were torches lit down the tunnel corridor every few feet. *As you wish,* the chilly voice spoke into her again, nearly causing her to flea to the side of her dragon.

No, she scolded herself and started down the ladder. It went on far longer than she ever would have dared let herself believe, but Iviana couldn't help being grateful she wasn't pulling herself up a rope. When she spotted a lit room beneath her, she dropped to the floor and immediately crumbled, exhausted from the trip downward.

Swiftly, she rose to her feet again. This was not the place to be vulnerable. No, this was the last place she could let her guard down.

The sinister presence in the air was stifling now as Iviana scrutinized the underground room. Silently, she pulled her sword from its scabbard, thankful she had been keeping herself familiar with it in her hut during her time on the island, and started forward. There were tables and shelves everywhere she glanced covered with books, vials, insects, herbs and items she couldn't put a name too. Lightly touching her fingers to one of the potted plants, she felt the kiss of death in it. This was the opposite of healing and her whole body convulsed from the mere touch of the wicked thing. She quickly continued her journey through the witch's chambers, but did not find the woman. There were so many rooms leading this way and that and Iviana began to feel lost and hopeless.

Finally, she recognized she was part of a game and shouted, "Enough, Aradia! Show yourself!"

"Ivi?" surprised voice called to her.

"Flynn?!" she screeched. "Where are you?"

"Uh, this way. I'll sing you a tune 'til you find me," he said, then began to sing in a surprisingly easy voice until she found him, behind bars, hands and legs tied.

"Oh, Flynn..." she muttered aloud and knelt before his prison.

Flynn smiled roguishly. "Iviana the dragon-savior, where have you been all my life?"

Iviana tried pulling at the bars, but they were steadfast. "What are you doing here?" she asked. "You are the last person I expected to find."

"You remember the witch I told you about? The one I asked for help when my sis' was ill? Turns out she's a *really evil* witch."

Iviana couldn't help letting a chuckle escape her lips. "No kidding?"

Flynn's face turned white as a sudden thought occurred to him. "Your dragon's not here is he?"

Iviana's stomach sank without knowing why and the answer showed on her face.

"Don't worry, lass," Flynn said, offering a half smile. "She may not know it. Speaking of, I think you ought to get your little hide out of here while you can."

"I can't... it's hard to explain. I'm... seeking."

"*Oh*, alright, go 'seek' elsewhere then, dear one. This lady's a kook. I haven't even been informed as to why I'm here yet and I've been here for months. She just comes in to gaze at my handsome face from time to time."

Iviana ignored the crack. "Trust me, I would like to leave," she said. "With every bone in my body, I would like to fly out of here, but even if I could, I'm not leaving you here. Where is she, anyway?"

He laughed. "You want me to grant you directions to death? I don't think so. Either get yourself out of here or you can sit and wait."

She raised her eyebrow at him and sat herself down on the ground, arms folded.

Flynn tried desperately to convince her to go while she sat, but she would have none of it.

"What do you mean you're 'seeking', anyway?" he asked. "Where have you been? I haven't seen you since I carried you out of that cave and gave you up to your dragon."

"You carried me out? I wondered why I didn't remember leaving myself. How did you know I was there?"

"Your dragon came to find me. He actually let me fly with him without you. I thought that was rather generous, but I suppose it was all for you. I don't know how long you had been in there." He hesitated before saying, "I'm glad to find you're alright."

"Thanks," she answered gravely. "I just wish I could say the same for you. How did you get down here, anyway?"

"It was after you and your dragon left me by the cave. I was going to go in and have a good look at that door, but something queer hit me and the next thing I knew, I was here in this musty cell: my current little home for far too long. How do you like my new look? I never thought a beard would suit me." He rubbed his chin on his shoulder. "But what do you think?"

Iviana glared at him and shook her head. "You're ridiculous. I'm going to go find–"

"No need," the cheerful, chilling voice of a woman interrupted.

∾22∾

"ARADIA," Iviana whispered, standing quickly to her feet.

"Who else would it be?" Aradia replied in a voice that was low and melodious, yet did not necessarily sound as though it was her own. "Now, who have we here?" She strolled up to Iviana and was about to hold her chin up for a better look, but the young Seeker stepped away from her.

"Don't touch me," Iviana said icily, wishing she hadn't re-sheathed her sword.

The woman clucked at her. "I so hoped you would come, my dear; a child of the Greater Archipelagos and the same I ventured upon at Jaela's Cavern... with the 'Great Tragor'," she mocked. "I hope you have brought him with you. Though, to tell you the truth, he's hardly what I need anymore."

"What do you need?" Iviana queried.

"Why, you, of course. I could smell the dragon a mile away and when I saw his rider, I thought, 'Aradia, why should we go through the trouble of capturing that foolish boy'"—she gestured to Flynn—"'and persuading *him* to retrieve what we need when we can simply use him to bring us our weapon.' Well, somehow you've arrived a bit earlier than I'd planned, but all the better I suppose. So... here you are, a lovely, *little* thing you are too. Look at those dainty features. They will suit me nicely." She grazed her hand over her own cheek.

Iviana realized then that this woman may have been the cause of Flynn's first abduction so many months back, but that was not the important issue at the moment. She squinted her eyes and asked, "What do you mean?"

"I mean, dear, little fool, I need only your heart to make it possible for me to pass through the door in Jaela's Cavern and into the Greater Archipelagos. I *had* formerly planned to consume the heart of a dragon to do so, but then I would have to take the form of one of those clumsy beasts and, to tell you the truth, the things make my mouth sour." A sinister laugh began to form in her words as she continued, "But I think returning as a lovely, young woman, nay, the *great-granddaughter of Latos*," she laughed harder, holding her stomach, "would be much more fun." She stopped her fit of laughter and looked directly into Iviana's eyes. "And to tell you the truth, I think I can do far more damage with your little human frame than that of a dragon."

Iviana smiled then. "I'm afraid your plan has a kink in it, Aradia."

The witch growled and a dark force shot from her body through the room, knocking Iviana to her knees. "I am never wrong," the sorceress hissed.

Iviana picked herself up. "Rarely ever," she corrected. "You see, they probably have about as much faith in me as they do in you after what I've pulled. They'll cast you out the moment they see you... or me."

Aradia began to laugh again. "It matters little. I have my *craft* to help me with little issues like that."

"Excuse me, ladies," Flynn spoke. "I really hate to interrupt, but would it be possible for one of you to fill me in?"

Before Iviana had a chance to note irritation flare upon Aradia's face, the witch conjured a translucent wraith and cast it upon Iviana who fell on the ground, crying in agony.

Aradia stood over her, saying, "Ah, just where I

need you, my dear."

Iviana couldn't move; she was paralyzed. *But that can't be,* she thought. *I have my gift.*

"Leave her be!" Flynn commanded, rising to his feet, despite his bound ankles.

Aradia froze and hesitated at his words, surprising all three of them. The witch looked at her hands and seemed to grow dizzy. *"WHAAAT is thisss?!"* she screamed.

The witch turned her attention from Iviana and darted toward Flynn, knocking him to the ground with her power, where he, too, was paralyzed. *"Do not speak again, halfwit!"* she demanded and turned back to Iviana who was beginning to realize the real reason she had been led to the lair.

"Flynn!" Iviana yelled. "Flynn, you have to help me."

He grunted through the pain of whatever Aradia had sent through him. "I'm a little tied up here..."

"No, you're so much more than you think you are. You're different, I think—more so than you could ever imagine..."

"What?" he called, bewildered and in pain.

"I'm not certain I understand it either, but I know I can't do this without you. Tell her... command her..."

"Command the quack? Are you kidding me?"

Aradia screeched and shrieked, shaking with anger. She snapped her fingers and a fire appeared beside Iviana. Nasty, obscure shapes dripping with iniquity formed within the flames, grasping for Iviana's flesh. They burned her, but she was frozen on the floor, held by Aradia's power.

She screamed in pain and whimpered with what strength she had, "Flynn..."

"Stop!" Flynn shouted with an authority he didn't know he had. "Put out your fire. I... I command it!"

Immediately the fire snuffed out and Aradia stared at the lack of it for a moment before turning herself on Flynn.

With Aradia's attention elsewhere, Iviana realized she was no longer paralyzed. Quickly, she chased after Aradia with her sword, but a translucent wraith surged at her, flinging her body mercilessly into the wall behind them and pinning her there. It breathed down her neck, taunting with a familiar voice, *You'll die here, all alone.*

Iviana looked beyond the cruel being and saw Aradia raise her hands in the air, as if about to strike. Searching for some way to save her friend, Iviana threw her sword to Flynn, shouting his name.

Flynn's attention diverted to the sword that sliced through the iron bars and landed, gleaming, at his feet. He half-smiled at the impossibility of it and managed to snatch the sword up to make a wild stab at Aradia, but she was too swift for him and dodged so that the only puncture she received was to her arm. The woman angrily clutched at her wound and screeched again, a thousand voices in unison. Her delirious tantrum granted Flynn enough time to shred his ropes and furiously slice through the iron bars.

Having gained his freedom, Flynn ran toward Iviana (who was beginning to wonder where Naphtali had gotten that sword), but Aradia came down on him with flaming eyes. The sorceress began to chant, sending a black, pernicious force coursing over him. He screamed until unconsciousness began to overtake him and still she did not stop, a mad fervor in her inflamed eyes.

Iviana struggled with the wraith that pinned her, but it persisted in its relentless assault. *No, no, you'll go mad before it comes to that,* it continued its taunt. *You're fragile, little Iviana.*

The words filled Iviana with the rage of a lioness. "No!" she snarled, surprising herself. *"I am not weak!* Those who trust in the One Eternal will gain strength." She struck her foot upon the ground casting a pulse through the floor and the earth around them began to quake.

Aradia ceased her attack on Flynn as the phantom screeched away from Iviana and fled into the witch. The aged sorceress began to tremble in fear. Iviana dashed forward and reached for the sword beside Flynn, making an attempt to behead Aradia, but a sword appeared in Aradia's hands and she parried. They continued the combat as the earthen walls began to crumble and disintegrate around them. The stories of soil overhead parted and collapsed around the three.

"We will have your heart, girl. We will have your heart!" the witch chanted with her thousand voices. "You will fall before us and we will destroy those whom the Great One loves. We will destroy you, chosen one."

The voices were grotesque and Aradia was lost in their frenzy. The mad gleam in the witch's eyes was fiercer still as the sword was desperately raised over her head, ready to be brought down on Iviana. But the Seeker was faster. She plunged her weapon into the witch's side and drew it out again, prepared for the final blow.

The earth surrounding grew still and silent and

the moonlit sky gleamed down upon them.

"Iviana, please," Aradia's voice returned to her, absent of the thousand voices that had been there previously. "Please, have mercy on me. You have freed me from the wretched hold of those monsters. You must help me. Have mercy on me." She sobbed into her hands.

Iviana hesitated. Aradia's voice was sincere and she could not bare to strike an innocent. Perhaps she could help Aradia find her way back from the dark path she had taken.

She knelt beside the woman and looked into her eyes. They were a rich brown now with no sign of flame. Laying her hand on the wound she had given her, Iviana spoke, "I think we can salvage it. You will not die, but I need your promise: a sacred promise. You must vow to give up your evil and follow the Great One."

"Yes, Iviana," Aradia said between sobs, "that is all I want..."

"Alright, then vow it."

"I,"—Aradia snatched Iviana's sword before she could stop her—"VOW IT!" The witch stood and kicked Iviana to the ground with the force of demonic power. Iviana struggled to stand and step out of the blade's reach, but as she did, her foot caught on a clump of fallen earth, tossing her to the ground.

Aradia laughed insanely, saying, "We will have you now!" when, suddenly, a creature appeared soaring down from the sky overhead. Iviana recognized him, but it was a few moments before the sorceress realized what had caught the Seeker's attention.

Finally, Aradia raised her head to the dragon and dryly whispered, "No, it cannot be."

Much closer now, the Great Dragon of the Ages opened his ferocious jaws, releasing a violent outcry and casting brilliant blue-white flame over the woman, reducing her to ash. The dragon floated down beside her ashes and released a long, hot breath from his nostrils, sending her away forever.

Tragor turned to Iviana who gawked at him, stunned. The Great Dragon cocked his head in question and the young woman awoke from her stupor and flew toward him. She held him in her arms as his wings slowly wrapped around her small frame and remained there for some time as tears of relief flowed over her soft cheeks.

❧23❧

IT WAS POURING rain when Flynn awoke to find Iviana and his sister, Laurel, standing over his bed.

"Flynn! I knew you'd be alright!" Laurel exclaimed, reaching down to give him a good squeeze. She added a light smack on his head. "I thought you were with Ivi!"

"'Be alright?'" he asked, confused. "I can't remember... What happened?"

"Do you remember being held in an underground cell for a while?" Iviana asked gently.

"Yes... I think so... kind of a blur."

"How about when I found you there and Aradia lost her temper with us?" Iviana asked again.

"Yes..." he answered. "It feels like a dream. How did we make it out?"

"Tragor."

"Eh?"

"Lets just say the ground parted for the Great Dragon of the Ages."

Flynn half chuckled. "Alright. I can live with that. I assume he brought us home then." He sat up, looked around and patted his sheets. "Mmm, it's good to be here."

"I'll run and get you some lunch," Laurel offered and left the room.

Flynn turned to Iviana, saying, "Well, my lady dragon-savior, I assume you'll be taking off without me again soon?"

"No. I'm going to wait until you are well enough to travel. I'm taking you on an adventure."

"Really?" he asked cheerfully. "Well, if it includes the dragon, I'm in... except..."

"Laurel is to be married," Iviana supplied. "We'll be here for that too."

Flynn sat up straighter. "What? That was fast."

"Not really; you were gone for some time and when a gentleman came calling soon after you left... well, they've had plenty of time to court."

"How long was I gone? And who is the braggart who thinks he can marry my sister without granting me a look at him?"

"Eh, that would be me." A gentle looking man

walked into the room. "And I can promise you we weren't going to wed until your return." He held out a hand to Flynn. "I'm Retrom, at your service."

"Sir Retrom of Galsbury Hall," Iviana added.

Flynn blinked. "Ah, what brought you to our humble house, Sir Retrom?"

"Just Retrom, please. It was a nasty storm that led me here. When Laurel, the darlin' she is, saw me riding through the village in the middle of a torrential downpour, she came running to offer her home to me until the rain settled."

"I assume you'll be taking her to your estate then?" Flynn asked, a little dazed by the thought. "Where might that be?"

"It's a few days ride north. I would be happy to make the trip with you when you're feeling up to it."

"Suits me fine."

Laurel entered with the meal for her brother. "You'll love it there, Flynn. The stables are nearly half the size of our little village."

"It's not so grand as all that," Sir Retrom assured.

"Well, I see a great deal has taken place since I've been, uh, away," Flynn stated, almost with a sigh. "I trust your decision, Laurel, and I think I like the man already, if it's worth anything."

"It means alot, Flynn," Laurel beamed. She

began to tear up and ran out of the room. Her fiance followed.

"Alright, then, Ivi..." said Flynn. "Tell me of this grand adventure."

After Iviana shared the whole of her stay in the strange realm of the Greater Archipelagos, she broke the news she'd been dying to share with him.

"When we were in Aradia's lair, and your words had such an uncanny affect on her actions... I realized that you had a Great Gift and that there was actually a reason we kept running into each other. You were truly the one I was seeking. You are the next Realm Leader of the Greater Archipelagos."

Surprisingly, Flynn struggled to believe not in the existence of another world, but that he could possibly be the next chosen leader of it, chosen by some mysterious being called the Great One.

"I don't understand," he said. "Am I supposed to be related to these people somehow?"

Iviana nodded. "I can't say how, but I'm guessing it's in your ancestry somewhere along the line."

"It *would* explain why that crimson door in your cave gave me the willies. Felt like it was calling to me. Guess some part of me knew it was familiar. I didn't get a chance to try it, though. Boy, would I have been shocked by what was on the other side."

"It *called* to you? It wouldn't even let me through."

"Why ever not?" Flynn seemed irritated by the fact.

"Nimua—a friend of mine—said they don't allow people to enter the realm who haven't been born there even if they're kin—at least not without permission. Maybe the door knew it... somehow."

"How could a door *know* something like that?"

"I don't know. There's a lot about that door I don't understand. Actually, the whole realm is still a question in itself."

Flynn suddenly looked a little shocked. "Ivi..." he said.

"What's the matter?"

"Do you think I could have been born there then?"

"I–I suppose so. You would know better than I."

"I don't know. My parents were rather odd people, now I think about it, and they weren't altogether forthcoming, I remember, though they were warm. At any rate, they died when I was twelve. They never said anything about, well, you know... another world."

"Now I wish you could have tried the door, just to be certain."

"I know. But, Ivi, how do you know that *I'm* supposed to be this great leader?"

She shrugged. "My gift... and yours. I guess they would call you a... a Speaker, perhaps. Like I said, when you spoke to Aradia, she listened, as if she was doing so against her will. Your words had surprising power and I just knew. The Seeker's fire was what had been leading me to you, to Tragor and to the Greater Archipelagos. I just never realized it."

"But... why *me?* I didn't know the place, *some other universe*, existed until now and lets just say, I don't think I'm exactly leader material."

"Apparently, the Great Once thinks otherwise."

Flynn heaved a breathe in. "I suppose I'll have to speak with this Great One then and give Him a good talking to."

Iviana smirked. "I don't know if you're aloud to do that, friend."

❧

That night, Flynn had a dream in which a mysterious winged messenger of the Great One shared some of what the Great One had in store for him. He refused to share anymore with anyone, but

303

it seemed to change his person and everything he had previously believed.

He confessed to Iviana that he was willing to travel with her to see this land, saying, "I suppose you may be right about my calling... and I will try to live up to it."

"Good lad," Iviana replied.

The next couple of months consisted of recovery and wedding preparations, until the blessed day arrived. Laurel wore an exquisite white gown and was drenched in flowers and jewels from head to toe. Her smile glowed brightly when she strolled down the isle toward her betrothed, whose smile shown just as bright.

"If it were any man but him, I could not bare giving her up," Flynn told Iviana after the ceremony, while he packed his things for their journey.

They stayed that night at Sir Retrom's estate and the next morning were waved goodbye by Laurel and her new husband.

"I wish you were coming with, Laurel," Flynn said when he hugged his sister goodbye.

"Me too," she told him. "I may visit someday, if they'll have me."

Flynn hopped on the dragon before Iviana had a chance to. "You ready, beasty?" he asked. Tragor snuffed smoke into the air. "Maybe you ought to hop on Ivi..." Flynn said hesitantly. "Quick."

Iviana laughed and hugged her friends before leaping onto Tragor's back. The two shouted farewells as the dragon lifted off the ground, his great wings stirring the ground beneath them

.

✌24✍

"WHAT *WAS* THAT THING?" Flynn asked breathlessly after they were thrown out of the swirling vortex.

"I don't know," Iviana answered simply. "My guess is it's the only way a dragon can get from one realm to the other since they can't fit through the door. I have yet to inquire about how it all works."

Flynn gasped when he saw the view of the Greater Archipelagos below him. "My... isn't that grand."

Iviana agreed.

"It's even prettier than Laurel's eyes... and your curly hair." He gave it a tug.

"Not that pretty."

"Which island are we headed for?"

"It's the northern-most island so it's not in view

yet. Give him a few minutes; we'll be there soon."

When at last they landed on the shore of the Isle of Dragons, Flynn danced around in the sand shouting his excitement. Unable to believe he was truly in another world, he ran over to the water and gasped before lapping some of it into his mouth.

"This is delicious!"

Iviana bent and drank some as well. It did taste good.

"Like honey," Flynn commented.

"Ivi?" a voice spoke, rising out the water.

Iviana jumped. "Oh, Nico!"

"Uh, what are you doing here?" Nico asked her. "I'm fairly certain you've been banished."

Flynn looked at Iviana quizzically.

"It doesn't count until they've said it to my face," she decided.

Nico froze when he saw the man Iviana had brought with her. "They're not going to like that," he said.

"They had better," Iviana retorted. "He is the next Realm Leader of the Great Archipelagos."

"Oh... so you found him. From which island do you come?" Nico asked him.

"Er, it's hard to say..." Flynn replied.

"Nico," Iviana interrupted. "Do you know

where Naii is?"

"I think she's with the council right now."

"Thanks. Come on, Flynn."

Nico ran and stood in front of them. "I wouldn't do that, Ivi. Wait until Naii's at home... alone."

Iviana ignored him and marched toward the Hall of the Council.

※

The doors of the council hall flew open by the might of Iviana's hands and she strolled directly to the middle of the great room. Flynn followed closely behind.

The room was stunned silent until Naii recognized who had entered. "Iviana!" she shouted, relieved to find her alright.

Iviana smiled at her and mouthed, "I'm sorry."

Kurnin stood to his feet. "That *girl!* Quickly, grab her!" he commanded.

No one moved. All were looking to Rhimesh for what was to be done. She sat quietly smiling. "Kindly take your seat, Kurnin," she said absently as she looked directly at Iviana. Then she asked, "I trust you had a pleasant trip?"

"Yes."

Rhimesh gestured to Flynn, who was behind Iviana. "Who is this you have with you?"

"Oh, this is Flynn." Iviana stepped aside to grant the Realm Leader a clear view of the tall man.

He gave a gallant bow to the ageless woman.

"He is not an islander?" Rhimesh asked.

"He has not grown up in the Greater Archipelagos, no."

Gasps filled the room as they realized the law that prohibited an "outsider" to enter without express permission had been broken twice within the same year.

The smile on Rhimesh's face did not fade. She asked, "What is his significance here?"

Iviana took a step forward, looking only at the Realm Leader. "I have used my Seeker's gift... and have found the one who is called to be the future Realm Leader of the Greater Archipelagos."

Kurnin smashed his fist against his armrest and shouted, red-faced, "This is an outrage!"

The room filled with shouts and murmurs just as it had the first time Iviana had been in the hall, though twice as loud.

Naii gave Rhimesh a pleading look and mouthed, "Rhimesh, please."

Rhimesh's booming voice filled the room, "Alright. Settle down, settle down." The council immediately grew quiet at her command. "Iviana, will you please tell us of your journey? I would dearly like to hear about it."

Iviana nodded. "The night I left, I followed my gift... the burning..."

Kurnin stood and shouted at her, "And why did you leave without permission from your council?"

Rhimesh waved a hand at him and he sat down, but Iviana turned to him. "You are not my council. Therefore, I did not need permission to leave. Had I waited for it, however, I know full well I would never have been aloud to use the gifts the Great One has bestowed upon me." Kurnin looked to Rhimesh for permission to respond, but Rhimesh ignored him and waited on Iviana to continue.

"I followed my gift and it led me to the... what do you call it?"

"Portal?" Rhimesh supplied.

"To the portal and into my home world. Once there, I was led to the lair of Aradia-"

"Impossible!" someone yelled.

Rhimesh raised her brows in surprise. "She is alive?"

"No," Iviana answered, "but she was. It seems she

had spotted Tragor and me with this man." She gestured to Flynn. "She used her craft to kidnap and hold him within her home." She relayed the story of Aradia's plot and eventual defeat.

Kurnin started again, trying to keep his voice calm so as not to be scolded again. "You... expect us to believe that you two have managed to defeat the witch that succeeded in stealing the life of the Great Warrior, Latos, even with the Great Tragor at his side?"

"Circumstances played out differently in our case," Iviana answered plainly. "We could not have done it without the help of the Great Friend—I mean, the Great One." She regretted her slip.

"Blasphemous!" Kurnin roared. He stood and marched over to Iviana. "Even if this string of lies were true, Rhimesh is healed and," he turned to the council, "the girl disrespects this fact and curses her reign as Realm Leader by bringing *this* boy to us."

Rhimesh did not stand or add to the show Kurnin was creating. She simply sat with a restful smile on her face and spoke, "Iviana was the one who provided my healing."

The whole room was a circus of outbursts. Even Naii looked surprised at the news.

Rhimesh proceeded, "She is a powerful Healer

and a gifted Seeker from the sound of it -"

"But she lies!" Kurnin shouted in an irritating, high-pitched voice that Iviana never dreamed could come out of the big, bearded man. "No one has ever been granted more than one gift before—except that *Marquen*."

Iviana was surprised at this information, but was distracted when Rhimesh gave Kurnin a cold glare, silencing him, and said, "We would be wise to embrace her and we would be wise to embrace this Flynn, I think." She waved a hand, absently saying, "Council dismissed." Then she stepped from her chair and said, "Flynn, I would like to speak with you alone, in my home. I'll meet you there in a few minutes." She immediately waltzed out the back door, before any member of her council had a chance to protest.

Flynn gave Iviana a look of surprise and shook his head as if he couldn't believe what was happening.

"Don't worry. She's not as intimidating as she appears," Iviana offered.

"Oh, I'm not worried about her. She's amazing. Did you see the way she handled those people?"

Just then Naii came up to them and quickly escorted them out of the building. "Lets get out of

312

here before Kurnin or one of his group eats you."

As they stepped onto the path outside, Iviana spotted Nimua and Darist running up to them. Darist scooped Iviana up and spun her around until Nimua yelled at him to put her down so she could hug her too.

"Thanks for the goodbye," Darist said.

"Sorry, I–"

"Don't worry about it," he stopped her. "At least we knew where you were, thanks to Nimua, who sure took long enough to fill us in."

"I wanted to give her time to look. I didn't know she'd left the realm!" Nimua defended.

Naii turned to Darist, asking, "Will you please show Flynn to Rhimesh's hut?"

Darist looked curiously at the man who had been standing there. He raised an eyebrow and put an arm over Flynn's shoulders, escorting him away. "So, you're Flynn, huh?"

"Mhm. Darist, I take it?"

"Yep. You attempted to kill a dragon? That's twenty years bad luck, ya know."

"Is it?"

"Naw..."

Their voices trailed away and Nimua lowered her voice to say, "Oh, he's dashing, Ivi..."

Her mother broke in, "Nimua, not now." She looked around at all the staring faces. "Lets get her home."

༒

The next few weeks, Rhimesh skillfully worked on the council until they were open to the concept of Flynn being her eventual successor, though they did not care much for his gift. It seemed to intimidate them. Even so, everyone recognized that Flynn must have done something right because the Realm Leader invited him to accompany her in everything she did, allowing him to swiftly learn all he possibly could about the islands and what it was going to take to be leader over the entire realm one day.

Iviana and her friends teased him for being pet to the Realm Leader, but Iviana knew Flynn's position aided in making her more accepted in the eyes of the realm. Her friendship with the Realm Leader's favorite was an advantage that couldn't be ignored. It also helped that Kurnin was quietly removed from his position as Island Leader and replaced with Naii, another factor that didn't damage

Iviana and Flynn's standing in the community.

When things had been as sorted as they could for the moment, everything seemed to fall into semi-normalcy. Nimua and Darist chose this time to clue Iviana in on their relationship.

"You're kidding!" Iviana exclaimed. "Who have you told about this?"

"No one," Darist replied with a smirk. "Nimua would prefer to keep it quiet until she's able to wrap her head around the horrific thought of marrying me."

"Oh, it's not quite like that," Nimua defended. "We simply agreed we wouldn't promise ourselves off to anyone else... without talking to the other first, at least. I suppose that makes us a little more than just plain old friends... wouldn't call it an engagement though." She winked at Darist who shrugged at Iviana.

And, though the couple spent more time together than they had before, Iviana had trouble wrapping her own mind around the relationship. It was a struggle to see it succeeding if Nimua persisted in gushing about how charming and handsome Flynn was. Iviana scolded her for this one day, but Nimua would have none of it. "Oh, don't be so bitter, Ivi, just because Nico and Leilyn are engaged."

Truth be told, Iviana was happy that Nico had found another to care for. She'd always known his feelings for her were shallow and she only hoped the two were going to make each other happy. Besides that, it helped Leilyn overcome her dislike of Iviana, now that she was engaged and not running around after Darist.

Yes, things were settled fairly for her, Iviana realized one afternoon when she was on her way to meet Tragor, who was waiting for her on the beach.

"Where are you going?" Flynn's voice asked behind her.

She turned around to face him, her travel bag packed on her back. "I'm going home."

"Home," he tried the word on his tongue. "I thought you said you didn't have a home."

"I don't. I have a house and I'm going back."

He wanted to stop her but knew better. With a sad, half smile he spoke, "Well, I think it's safe to say, I'll never forget you, dragon-savior."

"Good. I wouldn't want you to. Perhaps, I'll come back and visit someday."

She turned to go, but Flynn stopped her retreat, asking, "In what village is this house?"

"FairGlenn." She smiled. "Goodbye, Flynn."

Tragor flew Iviana from the realm of the Greater Archipelagos and into the world she still did not know, but where her mentor had raised her from a child into a young adult. Leaving was not altogether easy, though it would have been if she knew she had her mentor to go home to.

Even so, she would not fear. That is what she had learned: not to fear. It was what Marquen had told her when she said her goodbye to him before leaving the realm: "Do not fear." It was a command she would take into her heart and never let go of.

But she was not necessarily unafraid now. She simply forced herself to not dwell on those things that made her heart heavy and she did not want to use fear as an excuse to leave her mentor's home. She knew she could not remain in the island realm anyway. They had been willing to accept her for her friendship with Flynn, Naii and Rhimesh, but somehow they had found it impossible to overcome the Great Gifts the Great One had given her.

Besides that, she felt deep inside that there was something left unfinished in her childhood home and she felt herself being called back. She was certain the Great One was the One calling her, though she did not know why.

Seek me. I am waiting.

❧25❧

"WE WONDERED WHERE you'd gone. The villagers haven't known what to do without Naphtali."

"Nonsense. They always knew 'what to do' without Naphtali or myself," Iviana replied matter-of-factly.

The young widowed woman, the girl who had been Iviana's only childhood friend for no more than a day, cast her eyes downward. "I know," she said, laying her hand upon Iviana's hand. "I'm very sorry for your loss, Iviana."

Iviana looked into her eyes and smiled gratefully. "Thank you, Merri."

A friendship developed after that and a true one. Iviana learned that Merri had come that day because she was worried. She had heard that the villagers had found a grave beside the cottage and Iviana was missing. When there were signs that someone was within the cottage, Merri felt she must stop in for a visit.

Merri promised she would return the next day and she continued to visit often in the days that followed. Some days she would come accompanied by her three children and other days would invite Iviana to her own home where she would spoil her with sweet breads and meats.

As time passed, and Tragor left his hiding place in the woods to return to his home, Iviana discovered that she didn't feel so lonely anymore. The quiet that had laid like an eery blanket over her mind before was now a sweet solitude and she knew she was not truly alone anymore.

The Great One spoke to her daily and, in time, Iviana came to depend on His company. The moment she awoke in the early morning, she knew He was there and she bid Him good morning. She always felt He replied with joy and urged her to hurry and see the new day He had brought her.

Even the animals came to visit again and surrounded her with their company, wanting to be near the Great One's invisible presence.

One day, Iviana awoke to the realization that

she had friends now: the Great One, who put all to rights, the forest animals and the villagers, who were miraculously melting to her presence in their community.

This became apparent one afternoon when, while Iviana sat in the warm grass milking her cow, she spotted a man carrying his daughter up the walk to her home. She stopped her milking, patting the cow to encourage it on its way, and met the man at the front stoop.

The man looked down helplessly at his unconscious daughter who lay in his arms. "Can you help?"

"We'll see. Bring her in." Iviana invited him to lay the girl upon a couch and asked what had happened.

"I don't know," he answered, brushing his fingers worriedly through his tousled hair. "We were gathering walnuts and then... she took my hand, saying everything was going dark. I told her to lay down, but she couldn't seem to hear me... and then she collapsed."

Iviana smirked at this. "It's alright, good man. She'll be alright and will soon wake. She's only fainted. The only worry we have left is why." She remembered back to her mentor's fainting spells and prayed this girl's case was not the same. "It's a hot day, that's a factor. How long have you been out in this heat?"

"All day until just before I arrived here. We're planning to sell the walnuts on market day and were wanting plenty."

"I see. How much water has she had while you've been out."

"Er, none at all, that I can recollect. Why? Is that bad?"

"Yes and no. It's nothing to worry about. In fact, be grateful. It means the lack of water is all that caused her to faint. Have her drinking plenty of water from here on out and she'll be fine." As she said this, she fetched a vial of smelly liquid and placed it under the girl's nose, waking her.

"Daddy, where are we?" the girl said dreamily.

The man embraced the girl, "Oh, Taia, we're in a very kind lady's home." He turned to Iviana saying, "Thank you. I remember when I was a boy, Naphtali saved my mother from what would have been certain death. I'll never forget her."

The man's words pleased Iviana more than anything in the world could, save her Great Friend. She knew it must be her Friend who caused the change in the community's attitude toward her and her late mentor. The community that made her cold and afraid formerly now warmed her with the multitude of love she felt pouring over her everyday. It was a love she never dreamed she could have and an acceptance from the Great One that made her place in this world so, so dear. For as He was so tightly tucked in her heart, so was she, even more so, in His. The reason for this was unknown to the Healer-Seeker-Seer, but she did not need one. She simply relished it.

She was thinking about these things while working in her garden one afternoon. She was pruning the climbing roses that were trying to block the entrance to her front door. As she carefully wedged her arm behind the sticky branches, a feeling like something exploding in her heart jolted through her in an instant, causing her to scrape herself on the thorny thing she was fighting.

Immediately she knelt to the ground and held her heart until it settled.

Yet even after the effects of the jolt had completely passed, she could not keep from weeping, for she knew it was not her own body that suffered. Rather, it was the heart of another that had stopped altogether. She remembered now the words Rhimesh had spoken to her long ago. The ageless woman had conveyed that when the Realm Leader of the Greater Archipelagos passes, no islander can escape the knowledge of it.

For information about this author,

visit **www.CassandraBoyson.com** or

like Cassandra Boyson on facebook.